Don't Go Down To The Woods Today

Ian Searle

The characters portrayed in this story are all fictitious. Any resemblance to real persons, living or dead, is completely coincidental. The settings described are also invented.

First published in 2019 by CompletelyNovel.com

ISBN 9781787234130

My thanks to Margaret Ingles, George Walker and Rachel Edwards for proof-reading.

PART ONE

An uneasy peace

I

Martha Brewer, postmistress, sipped her morning tea and kept watch over the village. Hartsfoot Post Office was ideal for the purpose. It was a brick-built extension to the old cottage, opposite the Coach and Horses. Between these two establishments ran the main road from Hazlehurst in the north to Woodbury on the other side of the Downs. At this point lanes ran east and west to form a crossroads. Windows on all three sides of her little shop gave Martha an excellent view, except for the stretch of road to the south. Immediately behind her in that direction lay a derelict plot which had once been the site of a filling station. The old pump, now rusting, still stood there like a memorial. The plot in question, Martha knew, had recently been sold, but to her intense frustration she had been unable to find out to whom.

Across the road she saw George, landlord of the Coach and Horses, sweeping the pavement as he did every morning. He looked up and to his left. He must have heard the lorry which now approached very slowly, and which passed annoyingly out of Martha's sight. By the way George was looking, it must have parked, probably on the vacant plot. After a couple of minutes George resumed his sweeping, but down the lane opposite her Martha now saw the familiar figure of the Vicar, the Reverend Graham Dampier, approaching on his bike. Dampier, a funny name, she thought. Most names ending in er, like her own, Brewer, were understandable; they stood for work that people did, brewing, thatching, farming. But Dampier, what kind of occupation was that about?

The Vicar dismounted when he got to the main road. He saluted George. Instead of crossing the road in front of the post office and going on to the Vicarage, he pushed his bike over to the front of the pub and began talking to George. Doubtless they were talking about the lorry.

The sound of a motorbike drew Martha's attention away from the two men. Noisy machines, motorbikes, she muttered to herself, as it appeared from the Hazlehurst direction. It had a sidecar attached. It, too, slowed down as it passed the post office and the noise stopped soon afterwards. Now her curiosity was fully aroused. She seized a broom, opened the door, with its Black Cat advertisement stuck on the glass, and went outside to sweep the pavement. From here she had a view of the next-door plot. If she strained her ears, she could hear what was being said.

"You need a hand?" It was George, shouting across the road. The vehicle was a tired-looking furniture van. The back was open. Two men in coat-overalls and a third in a worn, sheepskin jacket, were standing on the sloping tailboard. The man in the jacket was scratching his head, as though trying to work out a problem.

"Thanks," this man replied. "This is very heavy. Be careful it doesn't run away with us."

Now, even the Vicar was getting in on the act ,as he limped across the road to join them. The five men were huffing and puffing as they manoeuvred a large object, which looked like a piece of machinery, mounted on wheels, down to the ground. Martha had no idea what it could be.

"It's a lathe," said the man in the jacket. He held out a hand first to George, then to the Vicar. "Duncan Frome," he said.

"A lathe? You opening a workshop of some sort, are you?" George was naturally as interested as Martha.

"I hope so. I need to get the building up to scratch first."

This was interesting indeed. Martha continued sweeping, her ears still pricked. The building, the only one on the small plot which this Duncan Frome had bought, it seemed, was the old, flint-built smithy. It had served as the village blacksmith's workshop and forge until the mid-1930s. Arnold Grace had bought it then, and installed the petrol pump, but he had died in 1938. His widow had died four years later, and this plot had been up for sale ever since. The Old Forge was a romantic - looking relic, but it was in a dreadful condition. If the new owner intended to use it as a workshop, he would need not only to repair the roof, but three rotting windows and the door. As for the walls – well, they looked sound enough, but they probably needed work doing to them. And where was this newcomer going to live? The answer, at least in part, came quickly.

"We've got your room ready," George said. Nobody ever stayed at the Coach and Horses, even though it was an inn, as its name suggested. Hartsfoot was the kind of village people passed through without stopping. Those that had any business here, lived in the village. At least half the cottages had doors and window frames painted green, the colour of the Estate. The others were privately owned or rented, like the row of council houses that lined the road leading to the watercress beds and Manor Farm.

Martha was forced to retreat with her broom in order to serve Mrs Riley. Afterwards it would have been too obvious to resume her observations. She kept an eye on the front of the pub, and was rewarded by the sight of Duncan Frome following George into the side door, carrying a dilapidated suitcase. Shortly afterwards, she saw the furniture van return, on its way to Hazlehurst.

At 12.08, dead on time, the bus arrived, its diesel engine throbbing and bodywork rattling as though loose, as it stopped to allow a passenger to alight. Martha watched. A young man in a tight, blue suit stepped onto the road. He carried a small suitcase, and there was something about the way he carried himself that was familiar. As the bus drew away, he turned towards her. Of course, Arthur White, back from the army!

He would be about twenty-five now, she thought. Yes, he had been gone more than four years, and when he had gone to join up, it had been with reluctance, or so she had heard. Not for him a sense of duty, just a law he couldn't dodge. He had always been something of a tearaway, even as a boy. His father, Reuben, was gamekeeper, and lived in the keeper's cottage over a mile to the east, halfway to the village of Belham. Reuben White had avoided call-up for himself, though how, she did not know. Surely gamekeeping was not a reserved occupation, like farming? Maybe it was, because Reuben was Arthur's only living parent. More likely the Estate Manager had described his occupation as farming. Not that Martha knew Reuben well enough to ask him. She had heard some really unpleasant rumours about the gamekeeper. He wasn't very attractive to look at, but it was said he had an eye for the ladies.

What she and everyone else did know was that Reuben's son, Arthur, was a handful. He had been a real trial as a small boy, always in trouble. He left school at fourteen and went to work on the Estate. His father was busy there, still raised pheasants, and looked after the wood, known as The Chase, where he raised them. Arthur spent four years doing whatever the Estate Manager told him, whether it was hedging and ditching or helping repair Estate buildings. He had a poor reputation, even while he was working at these tasks, but the Manager felt constrained to put up with much of his bad behaviour. rather than risk losing the gamekeeper. That, at least, was the only explanation there could be for not sacking him. The Manager, Scrivener, grumbled and scolded, but kept him on. When Arthur reached the age of eighteen and was obliged to join up, it had been unwillingly on his part, but it had been a relief for others, including the Manager, and quite possibly for his father.

Arthur pushed open the door of the shop. "Got any change?" he asked.

"What kind of change?" Martha did not take kindly to his rude manner.

"Pennies for the phone."

She gave him nine fat copper coins and a threepenny piece in exchange for a shilling. He left without thanking her, and she watched through the window as he used the phone box. It was a short call, after which he picked up his case and walked over to the pub.

Martha had another puzzle on her mind: demobilisation was taking a long time. The war had been over two years now, and Arthur White was one of the first to return. However, Joe Champion, another man who had left the village at the beginning of the war, had been demobbed within two months of the announcement that the war was over. Why, she wondered, was there such a difference? It was not as if Joe Champion had been released on health grounds; he looked healthy enough. Perhaps there was no reason to it at all. Perhaps it was just that the Army worked in a mysterious way. The Army had not done Hartsfoot a great favour in releasing Joe Champion early. No one liked him. He was known as a wife-beater and a bully. Most people in the village steered well clear. Martha also wondered what he was up to. Rumour had it that he had found himself a job of sorts in Brighton of all places. At least that would mean he would spend less time in the village, and that must surely be quite a relief for his wife, Peggy, as well as his son, Percy. As for Percy, growing up without a father might have been the reason that he was so badly behaved. On the other hand, of course, it could simply be that he had inherited his father's bad attitude; "like father, like son" didn't they say?

II

It was the following morning that a truly interesting titbit came Martha's way from the postman, as he called in after doing his round of the village. He had called at the Frosts' farm earlier.

Only Dorothy Frost lived there now, and she made very rare appearances in the village.

After witnessing the end of the war in Europe, Albert Frost, Dorothy's father, died. The Frosts ran a small, arable farm on the outskirts of the village, adjoining The Chase, but they kept themselves to themselves. When Albert died, he left only his daughter to take over the farm. Dorothy was a strong woman, now in her thirties. She was in the habit of running the house ever since the death of her mother, ten years earlier. Between cooking and cleaning she worked with her father on the farm. Occasionally she needed to call at the post office, but she did her weekly shopping in the nearby town on Fridays, travelling in the old pick-up truck.

The older women in the village knew of her, and some remembered her as a schoolgirl before the war. She had been cheerful and bright then, a pretty girl, they all said, but her mother's illness seemed to have suppressed her ability to smile. In fact, she seemed almost to have become invisible once she left the village school at fourteen. No one remembered seeing her much after that, until her mother's funeral. A few villagers turned out for that sad occasion. Dorothy was there, looking not merely sad at the loss, but deeply miserable. They could only presume she had been very attached to her mother, who, in her turn, had not taken an active part in village life.

She wasn't very talkative after her father's funeral, though she shook hands with the people offering condolences. In reply to their enquiries she said she didn't know what she was going to do about the farm. It was clearly going to be too much for one woman on her own.

'Can you afford to get someone to help you?' she was asked, but she simply said, 'I don't know yet. It's a good thing we don't have animals to look after.'

Dorothy had a rough-looking dog, a couple of goats and a few chickens, but it was an arable farm: crops could survive a week or two without too much attention, whereas cattle would have been another matter. As for the goats, at a pinch they could be sold or slaughtered.

'I see Dorothy Frost has got herself some help with the work now,' the postman said. Albert's funeral had been three months ago, so the news was intriguing.

'Oh?' Martha was immediately alert. 'Who's that, then?'

'Don't know who he is. Just a young chap, can't be more than about eighteen. Suppose she won't have to pay him a full wage that way.'

'Is he living there?'

'Dunno, I suppose he could be.'

Martha began asking her regular customers if any of them knew about the new farmhand. No one seemed to know. The lack of information increased her curiosity, so that she asked Brenda, the Vicar's wife, if she knew about this new turn of events. Brenda knew no more than Martha. However, Brenda, in her turn, asked her husband, if he was aware of the young man; after all, he was a new parishioner. Graham was equally unaware.

"Brenda, dear," he said, "I'm not at all sure I'm the best person to call on Dorothy Frost."

"Oh, why do you say that?"

"She always seems on edge, whenever I speak to her. I seem to make her uncomfortable."

"You? Make someone feel uncomfortable? That sounds very unlikely. You get on with everyone."

"Usually, yes." Graham frowned. "I don't think it's my imagination. Of course, we don't know her very well. She and her father kept themselves very much to themselves. At the funeral I noticed she wasn't uncomfortable with me alone, either. Several of Albert's friends – male friends – spoke to her, and she was the same with them. She was almost shifting from foot to foot. She just doesn't seem at ease with men for some reason"

"Really? I didn't notice anything. She was fine with me. We spoke for a while about the farm and what she was going to do now she was on her own."

Graham looked thoughtful. He began filling a pipe. "Would you go to see her?" he said. "You could suggest she might like to join the Mothers' Union or the WI, encourage her to get out more, point out she might find it very lonely without her father."

"I don't imagine Albert was exactly jolly company," his wife observed with a wry smile.

"She probably does need someone to talk to," said Graham. "She must be grieving, whatever we think of Albert.

And I am a little concerned about this newcomer, a young man by all accounts, especially if he's living in the same house."

"Surely you don't think there's something going on?"

"No, of course not."

III

Brenda had always seen it her duty to help her husband in the parish. She was, in any case, curious to find out the truth about the new farmhand. So, the next day, she rode her trusty bicycle to the Frosts' farm. As she approached, a large dog, at the end of a long chain, barked loudly. Dorothy Frost appeared from a shed. In a sharp, no-nonsense voice, she told the dog to shut up. It did.

"Mrs Dampier!" she said, surprised. "Nice to see you. Is anything wrong?"

"No, we were both concerned for you out here on your own, so I thought I'd come and say hello."

"I'm fine," Dorothy said, "but, now you're here, let me give you a cup of tea. I made some fresh scones this morning."

Brenda was puzzled as she followed Dorothy into the kitchen and sat at the big, deal table. Dorothy did not look remotely like a woman weighed down by grief. There was a strange lightness about her movements, a smile on her face. She looked – Brenda admitted to herself – radiant. Brenda watched her almost skip into the old larder to fetch milk and home-made cream for the scones. An awful suspicion began to form: had Dorothy fallen in love? Was the rumoured new farmhand something else? Then the suspicion was mixed with anxiety, when she remembered the postman's comment, relayed by Martha, that the new worker was no more than a boy of eighteen. It was going to call for tact.

'How are you coping on your own?' Brenda asked.

'I'm not on my own any longer,' Dorothy replied, still smiling.

'Oh?' she pretended surprise.

'My son has joined me.'

'Your son!' Brenda had difficulty preventing her jaw from dropping. 'I had no idea you had a son.'

'He's been living with my aunt. She brought him up for me.'

'But -'

'It's a long story. My father wouldn't have him in the house, you see.'

The child had been born out of wedlock, then. That would explain things.

'What happened to his father?' she asked.

'He's not in the picture.'

'Doesn't know about him? What about your boy? Is he in contact with his father at all?'

Dorothy shook her head. 'No. He doesn't know who his father is, nor will I tell him, never.'

'Forgive me,' Brenda said, 'but do you think that is fair on either your son or his father?'

'Fairness has nothing to do with the case'

The reply was definite, even mildly aggressive. Brenda dropped the matter. 'How old is he, your son?'

'Jack? He's seventeen now, a fine young man.' She was obviously proud of him. So, thought Brenda, this had all happened seventeen or eighteen years ago. Maybe the boy's father had been killed in the war –but no, Dorothy had used the present tense; "He's not in the picture," she had said. So, the father must still be alive. This was a mystery; so many years, and such an important secret. She wondered how Dorothy had managed to conduct an illicit affair, when she would have been a very young woman all those years ago. Her father and probably her mother would have had very strict codes of conduct, and she could well imagine they would have told their daughter she must either leave home in disgrace or get rid of the child by adoption. She had chosen to give the boy up. The transformed woman she was drinking tea with must have nursed the grief of separation for all these years, and at last, now both her parents were dead, she could recognize her son and bring him home to live with her.

IV

Graham dropped in to see Duncan Frome later in the week. The lorry which had brought the lathe had brought other items, including boxes of tools and a workbench. There was also a ladder, and this was now propped against the side of the Old Forge. At the top Duncan was working on the roof.

"Good morning, Padre," he said and made his way carefully down to the ground.

"I won't take up much of your time," said Graham, "but I wanted first of all to welcome you to the parish..."

"Let me stop you there, squire," said Duncan, raising a hand. "Before you say anything, I am not religious, so don't ask me if I'm going to come to church."

"That wasn't exactly why I came," Graham replied quietly, "though I'm sorry to hear it."

"I'm sorry, but you will never convince me there is a God of love, not after this last war."

"I realize just how much evil there has been for all to see over the past few years," said Graham, "but that does not have anything to do with the argument."

"I don't want to argue with you, but you weren't involved directly. You can't possibly understand how bloody terrible the war was. If you'd seen the carnage at Monte Casino..."

"But I *was* at Ypres," said Graham.

At this Duncan inclined his head in respectful acknowledgement.

"In fact," Graham continued, "I came on a completely different errand. I understand you will not want to stay on at the Coach and Horses for ever."

"Well, no."

"One of my parishioners, Mrs Cole, is a widow, who lives on her own in a three-bedroomed house. She might like to offer you accommodation as a lodger. I have already spoken to her to find out how she feels about the idea. She has grown-up children, who have moved away, and I think she would quite like the company. Of course, it's up to you and her, but it might suit both of you."

"Thank you, it sounds good, provided that we get on. Thanks for thinking of it."

"All part of the service."

"Where is this place?"

Graham pointed him in the direction of Mrs Cole's house.

Changing the subject, Graham asked, "You intend to open this again as a petrol station, do you?"

"Probably. I have other ideas to start with. I'm not sure there is a living to be made out of selling petrol, at least not yet, while it's rationed, and my expertise is as a mechanic. I'm not sure how big a demand there would be for that either, but I expect it will increase quite fast with men coming back from the forces. They'll want to get around and I could start a motorbike agency. A motorbike is a cheap form of transport. But to start with I'm going to concentrate on ordinary pushbikes."

"Well good luck to you with that! The village needs something positive to aim for. It's not like London or any of the big towns here. Victory brought relief rather than great excitement. I think everyone feels a bit lost and uncertain."

"Well, I've got plenty to do here. I have to get this old forge watertight, and I'll probably need at least one large shed as well. It will take a week or two to get all this done. It takes e a long time to get organised. It's not only the red tape and form filling, it's getting hold of the right materials and, for that matter, the right people to do the jobs that I can't. I have managed to find a sign-writer, so you can expect my new business to show itself shortly."

V

A week later the Old Forge was already looking much tidier. Attached to the wall was a long board, painted black, and in red letters it declared "Frome's Motorcycle and Bicycle Workshop". In the local newspaper, and by word-of-mouth in the village, Duncan advertised his willingness to buy second-hand bicycles in any condition. As the days went by, it became clear that he was happy to pay for ruined bicycles, those whose wheels had been buckled beyond repair, as well as older, plain dilapidated bikes.

At first people were mystified, then they began to understand his purpose, to dismantle the broken bikes to salvage the parts. He stripped down everything which was not damaged, cleaning it and, when he had enough, he began to rebuild the parts into new bicycles. These he painted – he had some trouble obtaining paint, but he still had contacts within the army – and the result was a number of very good bicycles, which he sold at a reasonable price. The fact that he was a motorcycle mechanic also spread. There were at first only one or two motorcyclists who called for help or for minor repairs, but he did a good job and the news spread. Business began to pick up. There was no doubt, everyone acknowledged, he was good with his hands. If necessary, he could even make new parts.

He and Mrs Cole hit it off straight away. The only condition she imposed on him was that he should take off his boots at the door and not bring too much grease into the house. Her late husband had worked for the railways, so she was used to seeing a man return from work in dirty overalls, his face blackened sometimes with coal dust from unloading the trucks at the station, and she was perfectly able to accept that. In return Duncan paid her a modest rent and offered a modicum of reassurance that there was a man in the house again.

VI

One morning, in response to a phone call, Duncan climbed on his motorbike to drive to Hazlehurst in a minor emergency. Although he locked the door of the Forge, there was no time to worry about the bicycles which were beginning to accumulate outside. There were at this time about five of them, in various states of disrepair. Since their owners had been only too eager to get rid of them, it would seem very unlikely that anybody would want to steal them back. He was, therefore, .surprised on his return to see a young boy look up guiltily from this pile of miscellaneous junk at the sound of his engine. The boy ran and hid behind the Forge itself. What the lad could not know was that Duncan had repaired the fence behind the Forge, so there was no escape there. Duncan turned off the engine, removed his leather helmet and strode towards the building. There he found a young boy, about 10 years of age.

"What's your name?" he demanded.

"Percy." It was uttered in a defiant, almost insolent tone.

"Percy what?"

"Percy Champion." This time there was even a hint of contempt in the child's voice, as though suggesting that any fool would know that fact.

"Come out of there." The boy made his way past the back of the building, brushing against the fence. He wore a grey pullover with holes at the elbows, short trousers, and socks of uncertain colour which had fallen round his ankles. On his feet he wore scuffed boots, which had obviously not been cleaned for many days. Once out of his hiding place, he made as if he would walk away. Duncan grabbed him by the shoulder and pushed him against the side of the building.

"What are you doing here?" he asked.

"Just looking round. It's a free country."

"This is private property. It's my property. I don't want nosy little nippers like you poking around here, understood?"

Percy Champion did not reply. Duncan shook him lightly. "Do you understand?" The boy nodded sullenly. Duncan released him.

"I'll get my dad on you!" the boy said.

Duncan laughed. "Bring it on!" he said.

"My dad will do you for attacking me! He's a soldier."

Duncan laughed again. "Good for him!" and he turned away, but Percy wasn't finished. He bent over and picked up a length of wood and, had Duncan not seen him from the corner of his eye, would have swung it viciously at Duncan. He reacted instinctively and quickly, dodging the blow and grabbing the boy's arm with sufficient force to make him drop the stick.

"You're an aggressive little blighter, aren't you?" he said.

But Percy had been surprised and impressed by Duncan's fast reaction. "How did you do that, mister?"

"Your dad is not the only man who is a soldier," he said.

Percy, released from Duncan's grip, now took a step back. but still faced him, his bravado giving way to something approaching respect. "Sorry," he said.

"I think we understand one another," said Duncan. "Just don't come snooping around here again, okay?"

"Can't I come back when you're here? I wanna see what you're doing."

Duncan suppressed a grin. The boy was persistent, if nothing else. "This place is open to the public," he said, "but not to snoopers or thieves, understood?"

The boy nodded. "See you then," he said, and marched away without looking back.

VII

"Are you settling in?" Mrs Cole placed a large, appetizing plateful of food in front of her lodger.

"Yes, it's a slow business."

"What exactly are you trying to do?"

"Well, to begin with I'm going to operate a repair shop for bikes."

"Most people round here do their own mending; they have to."

"They won't have to any longer, but that's only the start of the thing," said Duncan taking a forkful of sausage. "I'm also collecting old, broken bikes and using them to make new ones."

Mrs Cole nodded approvingly. "That sounds a good idea".

"In time I hope to develop the business. Pushbikes are only the start of it; I want to run a little garage dealing mainly with motorbikes."

"Not sure that will be very popular. Noisy things, or they can be."

"I never thought to ask you if my bike is a nuisance."

"No, not really. I suppose it is a convenient way to get back and forwards. I was thinking more on the lines of when you are working on bikes in your old forge. I imagine you'll make quite a racket then."

"I suppose it will make a bit of noise," Duncan admitted, "but most of it will be inside the Forge and the walls are very thick, so it shouldn't disturb too many people."

"It'll be interesting to see what that nosy Martha Brewer has to say about that," said Mrs Cole with the slightest touch of malice, "And do you think there will be enough business?"

"You said it yourself, Mrs Cole. Motorbikes are a convenient and cheap way of getting around, without going to the expense of buying a car. I reckon a lot of the younger blokes around here will go for them. It's my trade, anyway."

"You've not told me a lot about yourself," she said, "and I don't want to be nosy. I suppose you learnt about motorbikes and engines and such in the army?"

"No, I learnt most of what I know before I joined up. I worked in a motorbike factory in Coventry before the war, did my apprenticeship there."

"Well I'm blessed! My daughter Emily lives in Coventry. It's a small world. What brought you down to Sussex?"

Duncan didn't answer immediately. A strange look crossed his face, and the old woman wondered if she had touched a sore point. For a minute or two the man made no attempt to continue eating, although he had begun the meal with obvious enjoyment.

"Sorry," said Mrs Cole, a little embarrassed, "it's none of my business."

Duncan took a deep breath. "I needed to make a new start," he said. "I had to get away from the Midlands: it's full of painful memories."

"It's none of my business," Mrs Cole repeated. "I'm sorry if I've embarrassed you."

When Duncan raised his eyes to hers, she was shocked to see his expression. Whatever memories he was referring to, the pain clearly ran deep. She did not know him well enough to offer him the compassion he clearly needed. She rose and turned to leave the room, but he lifted a hand to stop her. "You may as well know," he said. She sat down with foreboding, wondering what kind of confession she was about to hear. Was he in trouble with the law?

"I did very well in the factory," Duncan explained. "I really enjoyed the work, and, after my apprenticeship, I was all set to stay there for life. I married my childhood sweetheart, Audrey, and we were happy. I had a stroke of luck, because I managed to invent a gadget which improved the carburation. A clever friend advised me to register the patent. It cost a packet, and I had to borrow, but it proved worth it in the end, because one of the manufacturing companies bought the rights from me. They gave me enough to buy a little house and I still have some of the money, which I'm using here." He paused, remembering happier times. "Then came the war. I could have stayed where I was, in a reserved occupation, but I felt I had to do my bit. I left my wife in our home, and I joined up. They put me in REME and kept me busy."

Mrs Cole said nothing, but she listened. Perhaps, she thought, it might be good for him to talk. She had come to understand loneliness. She also wondered what had happened to his wife, and what had brought him to live in a different part of the country. Duncan told her bluntly.

"The house took a direct hit," he said. "Audrey, my wife, was killed outright. My parents lived in the house next door. They were killed, too."

"Oh, my dear Lord! How terrible!" Instinctively, Mrs Cole reached out and put a hand on his arm.

"Life goes on." It was said in a neutral, weary tone, like someone repeating a lesson. "I'd rather you didn't tell everybody in the village," he said. "It's not that I specially want to keep all this secret; it's just that I don't want it to be the subject of gossip."

"I shan't say a word," said the old lady. Then, briskly, she added, "your food is going cold. You need to eat. You want me to pop it in the oven to warm it up? I'll make a pot of tea while I'm at it."

Duncan sat dumbly as she removed the plate temporarily. He was still staring at the wall, not really seeing it, when she returned. She poured his tea. She left him, then, to his private thoughts. She came back to clear the table a little later. He did not move. She washed up the dishes and settled with her knitting in an armchair by the fire in the sitting room. She left the door open in case he would prefer the warmth and company there. A little while later, Duncan joined her, sitting in the big, old armchair opposite, and lighting a cigarette. Neither spoke for a long time.

At 9 o'clock she switched on the wireless and listened to the news. When it ended, Duncan stood up. "I'm for bed," he said. "Work in the morning." At the door he turned and added, "Thank you."

"What for?" She said. "It was only toad in the hole."

"I meant thank you for listening," he said.

"I know, boy. I know. I've got grown-up children of my own, and I know how important it is to have someone to talk to. Get a good night's sleep."

Left with only the cat for company, the old lady reflected on the confidences she had shared. It was a very sad story, but she felt, in an obscure way, privileged that Duncan had told her. She also felt a reawakening of her maternal instincts. Now that her own children were making their way in life, and needed her very little, perhaps this was a way in which she could help somebody else. Duncan Frome, with his strange accent, his enthusiasm for motorbikes, his ambitions for his little business, could well provide her with an alternative way to use her natural desire to be of support. If this evening was anything to go by, she could yet provide comfort to another human being. For the first time in a while she went to bed with something like hope instead of resignation.

VIII

Most of the men returning from military service arrived on the bus. Martha had the great satisfaction of being the first to see them arrive. Since very few people had a car or could afford to pay a taxi to bring them home from Hazlehurst, the nearest station which had a passenger service, their only means of coming to the village was by bus. One such arrival had been Joe Champion, Percy's father. He came home within a few weeks of the end of hostilities. The others were much later, as much as two years later. When she saw him step down from the bus with the army issue suitcase in his hand, Martha's reaction was less than positive. Joe was an unpleasant, swaggering bully of a man, or at least he had been, before he left, and Martha had no reason to suppose he would have changed. She and the women in the village were very aware that his wife, Peggy, had for many years suffered physically at his hands. Peggy seldom ventured out in the years before Joe was called up. Free of his presence, she began to take a more active part in village life, joining the WI and the Mothers Union. She enjoyed the company at their little gatherings, but she was timid, and took a less than active part. Before Joe's departure there were occasions when she dared not show herself in public, because, all too often, she bore bruises or a black eye to reveal something of the state of her marriage. Now, Martha thought , things would go back the way they were. Peggy would once more not be seen in the village very much. In that she had been proved right.

IX

Duncan Frome's original enthusiasm was a little blunted after a few weeks, during which he seemed to be spending far more money than he could possibly earn. He understood in theory that he needed to be patient and to invest. The Old Forge building itself would be fine as a workshop, but he needed more indoor space for storage. He set about building a large, wooden shed. The villagers watched with interest, sometimes tinged with admiration, because he made a very good job of it, and he was a hard worker. They kept their distance, not sure what to make of the stranger in their midst. From time to time Duncan looked up to find Percy Champion standing, four-square, watching. The boy even lent an occasional hand, passing a hammer or a saw. There was, thought Duncan, some good in the boy after all.

It took him three weeks to complete the new shed. He had already spent time laying a concrete floor. He took particular care in designing wide doors, ensuring they could be very securely locked. He was far too busy to do much else. Mrs Cole, in her motherly way, fussed over him in the evenings, when he came home very tired.

"You're working too hard," she said. "Why don't you spend an hour or two at the pub? You can't be making very many friends at the moment."

"This is the hardest time," said Duncan. "There'll be time for socialising later, always provided I can make this scheme work, of course."

Mrs Cole said nothing in reply. She was growing quite fond of this quiet man. He was hard-working and determined, polite and reasonably friendly. She understood he was still grieving for his lost family. She also thought he needed to mix more. He seldom smiled, though that could stem from worries about the future of his business.

X

Two unconnected events brought unexpected opportunity. He was working on the new building one morning, when he heard a bicycle entering the forecourt. He looked round to see Graham Dampier dismount and lean his bike against the Old Forge wall. He turned towards him.

"Got a puncture, Vicar?" he asked. "I need the work, even if it is for a man of the cloth."

Graham smiled. "I'm afraid not," he said. "I'm here on a different mission."

"Pity."

"I've come to ask you a favour. It's something you wouldn't have thought of yourself."

Duncan took out a packet of cigarettes and lit one. He didn't mind taking a break.

"We are in real trouble," Graham began. "We are one member short on the Parish Council and, if we don't manage to fill the vacancy in the next few days, we'll be taken over by the District Council. That would be a great shame, because we would lose control over some of the things that matter to us."

"Parish Council! I told you from the beginning I don't want anything to do with the church."

"Ah! No, I said the Parish Council. Don't confuse it with the Parochial Church Council. The Parish Council is like a lower level of the District Council, local government. We look after things like the recreation ground, help with the school, although there is, of course, a governing board for that. We can even suggest improvements – one of these days it would be good to get street lighting, for example. It's everyday things like that."

"Don't think I've got the time, not really," said Duncan. "What made you think of me?"

"Well, you've clearly got energy and your future, at least your immediate future, is going to be bound up with the village. And in any case, you would bring fresh ideas to help us, I'm sure. But the real problem is that we must find a new Parish Councillor in the next few days or lose the Parish Council itself. It's not exactly arduous: we hold meetings in the evening about once a month – sometimes less frequently – and they only take about an hour."

Duncan scratched his head. "I don't think this is really me," he said.

"Can I at least ask you to think about it? I can't give you much time, I'm afraid. It might even be useful to you, when you think about it."

"How would it be useful to me?"

"You would be taking an active part in the village, together with the four other members of the Council. That would surely be good for you. It would help them to get to know you better. They could be influential in helping you get accepted. Mervyn Hardcastle would be especially good as an ally"

"I take it you're one of the leading lights?"

"It's part of my job, I suppose," Graham said with a rueful smile, and Duncan saw just a touch of mischievous humour in the expression.

When Graham came back a few hours later, Duncan agreed to be co-opted onto the Parish Council, which was due to meet the following week. The meetings were held in a small, private room in the Coach and Horses. If they proved boring or pointless, he could always walk away, but Graham's point, that he would become to some degree integrated into the village itself, was quite valid.

XI

The second event occurred two days later, when, returning to his lodgings at the end of the day, he found a letter waiting for him. It was from a friend in Guildford. Duncan opened it, interested in news of his former comrade, and wondering how he, too, was readjusting to civilian life. As he unfolded the letter, a clipping from a newspaper dropped out. It advertised a large sale of army surplus material. His friend had underlined one section of the advertisement. The government was selling off second-hand vehicles, and, included among them, were eight motorcycles. The sale was a week ahead.

This could be the opportunity he was looking for. His friend offered to put him up overnight if he wanted to attend. When he put the letter down, Duncan thought very hard. Much would depend on the price the bikes attracted at auction. His capital was already running down, because he had so far earned very little from the few bits of work that had come his way, and from the half-dozen rebuilt pushbikes he had sold. It would be a gamble to invest in second-hand motorbikes, which he would need to work on before he could sell. If they did not sell, his enterprise could come to a virtual end. He went to bed soon after 10 o'clock, but lay awake until the small hours, trying to make a decision. When he woke the following morning, the die was cast. He wrote a hurried letter to his friend, accepting the invitation. He also decided to employ a young girl from the village, Jenny Marchant, to look after the petrol sales.

XII

The Parish Council meeting took place two days before he set off for Guildford. He found it hard to concentrate, but not much was expected of him at this, his first meeting, and his fellow councillors were grateful to him for volunteering. The Vicar introduced him to the three other councillors. One was the farmer, Matthew Stevens, who was affable but said little. The Clerk to the Council was a woman, a tall, well-dressed, elderly lady with a serious demeanour. When she spoke, Duncan thought to himself she had a plum in her mouth. Her name was Mrs Crabtree, and she lived in one of the larger houses. The fifth member of the Council was also elderly, but in contrast to Mrs Crabtree, he was exceedingly jolly. His name was Mervyn Hardcastle, and Graham explained that he looked after the finances and was "something of a wizard when dealing with money". Mr Hardcastle also lived in one of the larger houses. Duncan was to learn over time that he had been an important village benefactor. One indication of this arose when, in Any Other Business, he suggested it was a good time to resurrect the village cricket club which had come to an abrupt end when the war began.

"We no longer have a ground," said Graham.

"That's not really a problem," said Mr Hardcastle, smiling and relaxed. "We could use my paddock. I don't use it for anything except my two goats. For matches and, I suppose, for practices I could simply tether them so they're out of the way."

"A sort of but me no butts," Graham joked. Mrs Crabtree looked pained, but Mr Hardcastle laughed happily. "Well," he said, "what do you think?"

They agreed it was a good idea, although they would need not only to recruit a team, but also to find someone to act as groundsman. Mrs Crabtree was a little uncertain what was needed, until the men explained that the pitch would have to be carefully prepared, involving the use of a roller as well as much mowing.

"What about you, Mr Frome?" Mervyn Hardcastle asked. "You're young and fit; do you play?"

Duncan admitted that he had been known to play cricket for his works team a few years ago.

"Splendid!" The originator of the idea applauded.

When Duncan returned home, he realized he had almost enjoyed the evening. For some weeks now he had been working on his own for hours at a stretch, and to be in the company of others, however trivial the conversation, had been agreeable. Next time perhaps he might feel able to take more interest in the proceedings.

XIII

"Christmas is coming," Mrs Cole said casually one evening, her knitting needles clacking.

"Yes, I suppose it is." Duncan hadn't given it a thought. After a while he added, "I didn't think about it, but will you want the place to yourself?"

"What are you planning to do?" she said in reply. "Have you any plans? Are you thinking of going back to Coventry?"

"Now I've made a clean break I don't really want to go back at all. There is no one there any longer."

"No family at all?"

"No."

For a while Mrs Cole said nothing, busy with her knitting and her thoughts. Then she said, "You know you're more than welcome to share Christmas with us here. Ruth is coming from Luton. She has the week off. I hope you won't mind having her around. Emily, my other daughter, will be in Coventry with her husband and his family."

"This is her home more than mine. How can I possibly object? It's nice of you not to kick me out for the week."

"Bless me! As if I'd do that! No, I'll be glad to have you here. You've become part of the furniture. I'm sure you'll get on with Ruth."

"I'm sure I shall."

"There is just one thing." Mrs Cole stopped knitting for a moment, lowered her head and looked at him over her glasses.

"Christmas is on the Thursday this year. Ruth is coming down on the Monday, specially for the carol service on Tuesday. That will be the 23rd."

"Yes?" Duncan failed to see the relevance.

"The carol service is very special in Hartsfoot. Everybody goes. It's not just a carol service, you see. The schoolchildren put on a nativity play in the church as part of the service. I know you don't go to church yourself, but it would feel terrible if Ruth and me went and left you here on your own. If you are going to spend Christmas here, will you please come to the carol service? I wouldn't ask you to go to midnight mass, but this is different."

Duncan thought for a moment. The whole Christmas business seemed to him something of a sham, the re-enactment of a legend. As for the carols, well, there wasn't much wrong with a good old singsong, however nonsensical some of the words were. The main thing was that this was obviously a strong part of the village tradition, and it would be wise not to challenge it. Above all, he did not want to hurt his landlady's feelings. She had been very kind to him, and he was becoming as fond of her as she was of him.

"OK, it's a bargain," he said. "Thank you for letting me stay."

Ruth arrived late on Monday. She was tall, pleasant and self-possessed. Once Duncan had said hello, he made an excuse to go to his room to work, so that mother and daughter could have the sitting room to themselves for the rest of the evening. At breakfast on the Tuesday morning, Ruth announced that she had a sudden hankering to visit the Beeches. At first Duncan thought this must be the name of a family, but Mrs Cole explained, "It's a place just past the old Manor. There's a little wood, all beech trees, on either side of the track leading to the Downs."

"Sounds like a good reason to take a walk that way. Are you game?"

There had been an overnight frost, and the ground was still hard. They did not talk very much as they strode through the village, up the Manor Drive, skirting watercress beds. By the time they arrived at the Manor Farm, they were both comfortably warm. The pathway began to climb immediately and within a few yards they were into the beech woods. The branches were now bare of leaves and the slight breeze made them groan uneasily. The ground beneath was covered in leaf litter. At the edges of the pathway this was very thick. Ruth insisted on walking through it, taking delight in kicking the leaves in a shower in front of her. The trunks of the great trees rose on either side, smoothly green and grey, like man-made columns, until the first branches spread overhead. There was very little noise other than the creaking of branches and the stirring of the smaller twigs so that Ruth's kicking game created soft, whooshing sounds. Duncan joined in and they were soon laughing like children.

The track climbed through the trees for no more than a couple of hundred yards. Here the trees came to an abrupt end, as did the path itself, and a wooden gate gave onto the springy turf of the Down. They continued up the slope, the grass wet from the melted frost. The air was crisp but refreshingly clean and smelled of thyme. Their breath turned to little clouds of steam.

"I've missed this," said Ruth, opening her arms wide to indicate the space around them.

"Your mother thought you might get homesick and want to come back," said Duncan.

"No. I know there is a lot of space here, and I love the country, but, well, I think I'd feel trapped. I need to get out and do things, meet people, do something worthwhile. Do you understand what I'm saying?"

"I think so."

"This probably sounds silly, but you know what I've missed most about this place?"

"Tell me."

"Trees."

"Trees?"

"There's something about trees. It's hard to say what it is. Perhaps it's their permanence. Those beeches we just walked through are probably two hundred years old. They were there not only when I was born, and throughout my childhood, but they were there when my grandparents were living in the village. From our house you can see three great elms that have always been part of my life And the huge yew tree in the churchyard, they say, is at least six hundred years old. Then there's The Chase.."

"The Chase?"

"That wood down there," she pointed. "It's private property now, but it's really old, lovely. It's a pity you can't just walk through The Chase when you like. The trees are wonderful. They make me feel – I don't quite know how to say this – that some things will never change. I wanted to come back to the beeches today to reassure myself that the world as I knew it had not completely disappeared. Does that make any kind of sense?"

"Yes, I think it does. Everything has changed with the war. I'd never thought of trees like that, though. Perhaps that's because I was born and brought up in a city, a man-made place. One thing you can't deny is that all the bombing has certainly changed the towns. I suppose the trees, and the landscape too, seem a lot more permanent."

Their walk brought them down by another track to a five barred gate on which they both perched to drink the tea and eat cake they had brought with them. Duncan asked Ruth about her work as an ambulance driver. She told him how much she enjoyed the work itself, how she had learned basic maintenance as well as picking up skills which began with first aid, and they had taken her to a higher degree of competence in dealing with injured people. She enjoyed using her skills as a driver and attending to the patients in her care. She had also made some very good friends, and had she achieved acceptance in a world which was normally dominated by men.

"Mum seems to have grown quite fond of you," she told Duncan. "Thank you for being so kind to her. I think she was quite lonely until you came along."

"It's worked out well for both of us," he said. "We look after each other. I was really pleased when she asked me to stay for Christmas. I didn't want to go back to the Midlands. Mind you, she drives a hard bargain. I'm not really keen to go to this carol service thing tonight. I'm not religious. I tend to think the whole thing is humbug, from Father Christmas onwards. It's just a pagan celebration of the change of seasons or something, I think even the Romans celebrated it in some form. Still, it's only an hour or two and I think I can just about manage that."

Ruth laughed. "You'll probably enjoy it," she said. "Think of it as a village celebration. The church will be full, candles burning everywhere, and everybody will be in a festive mood. Lots of them will be there to watch their children perform the nativity play that's part of the service. Everybody enjoys singing the carols. Just enjoy it!"

They jumped down from the gate and continued their walk. They got home hungry, feeling much better for the exercise.

XIV

Late in the afternoon Duncan took out his best suit and a clean shirt. He had not worn a tie since his last visit to the bank manager. He brushed his hair, glanced in the mirror, and decided he would do. Then he went downstairs and waited for the two women. He could hear them talking good-humouredly. Ruth was ready first. She was wearing a neat, woollen, two-piece suit. Her stockinged feet were in sensible, flat shoes. She wore very little make up except for lipstick.

"It all right for you men," she said. "Whenever we women have to get into our Sunday-best we have to make all kinds of decisions about what to wear. I hate wearing skirts. I wear trousers every day. But I do draw the line at a hat. I'm afraid I'm going to wear another headscarf."

"I don't suppose anybody would mind if you wore trousers tonight."

"Oh, there would still be raised eyebrows. I don't mind once in a while, and this is a special occasion, a village tradition."

Her mother appeared.

"You both look marvellous," said Duncan.

Armed with torches, they set off for the church. There was a half-moon, and the sky was clear. It was going to be another frosty night, and it was cold, even early in the evening. As they passed the houses on their way, Duncan noticed that most of them had left the curtains open. In most of the windows there were lights and the rooms glowed. Sometimes there was the glimpse of Christmas decorations, the glitter of tinsel or of glass baubles. In one house a Christmas tree had been placed right in front of the window.

Although they arrived at the church twenty minutes early, it was already nearly full. Duncan recognized many of the faces in the congregation. There was a sense of excited anticipation and much animated conversation, conducted in hushed tones. Right at the front of the church, beneath the chancel steps, sat a large group of children in costumes, ready to perform. Nearby, keeping a watchful eye on them, the two teachers sat on chairs. Duncan told Mrs Cole quietly he would prefer to sit near the back, and they filed into a pew. They exchanged smiles and nods with mutual friends and neighbours.

The church was lit by candles, creating an intimate atmosphere, but not a great deal of light, and it was only a movement in the front on the left which drew Duncan's attention to the little organ. The movement came from a young boy who was working a wooden lever up and down to pump air into the bellows. The organist began to play, and the congregation fell silent. There was something charmingly simple and unpretentious about this amateur music making.

The music stopped and the Vicar walked to the centre of the lowest step. He welcomed everybody and gave a special welcome to the children at his feet before beginning the service with a prayer. Duncan felt mildly uncomfortable. When everyone was seated, Graham explained briefly the order of service. There would, he said, be a carol followed by a reading and a second carol before the children enacted the events of the very first Christmas Day. The play would be followed by a further five carols and readings and the service would end with prayers. The first carol would be "Once in Royal David's city."

After the second carol the congregation sank back on their pews with the rustling of clothes. The children stood up and moved into pre-arranged positions on either side of the space which was clearly to be used as the stage. Three small boys, wrapped in brown, woollen blankets, and with chequered tea towels as headdresses, sat to one side of the stage, cross-legged. Opposite them two small girls, all in white, stepped forward. They raised their right hands and spoke together, "Fear not, we bring you good tidings of great joy..." The story was unfolded with the naivety and charm that Duncan expected. He felt embarrassed; these children were being made complicit in a lie. It was, he thought, just like pretending Father Christmas would come galloping through the sky to bring them presents.

An older girl, perhaps sixteen or seventeen years old, stepped forward next and began to recite a poem. But Duncan stood up quickly and stepped into the aisle. He hurried to the door, trying to do so unobtrusively. He fumbled for a moment with the heavy latch, but soon he was outside. In the dim light of the moon and stars he took half a dozen steps to a large tomb, where he sat heavily as though winded and, burying his head in his hands, he began to weep uncontrollably.

He was aware only of deep anguish. The young girl had chosen a poem which he had last heard spoken by his wife. It was a moment of intimacy between them, when they were both in a trance-like state of love.

"And love will last, though we may die."

The lines pierced him like a knife, and he could feel the warmth of her in his arms, her breath on his cheek. He had been transported to a time of joy and hope, but he knew that it was not real, the hope had gone, and with it, joy.

Someone placed a coat on his shoulders. He realized he was indeed cold. He raised his head. Ruth was sitting next to him. Shocked by the distress in his face, she put an arm around his shoulders. She said nothing but drew his head down and nursed him like a child. He was making an effort to control himself, but he continued to weep for a while. At last the pain eased, and he took several deep, shuddering breaths of freezing air.

"I'm sorry," he said. He could say nothing more, he was now very embarrassed, but repeated, "I'm sorry."

"There is no need," she said. "Whatever the trouble is, we obviously shouldn't have brought you tonight. Are you warm enough?"

He pulled the coat closer round him. He sat up straight, found a handkerchief in his trouser pocket and blew his nose. Then, from his jacket pocket he took out a silver cigarette case and took a cigarette.

"Can I have one, please?"

They sat in the cold churchyard without talking. Down the path, near the southern end of the church, the dark mass of the old yew tree loomed, and further down the hill, near the stream, the fan-shaped, leafless branches of tall elm trees were silhouetted against the starlit sky. From inside the church came the sound of another familiar carol,

"The hopes and fears of all the years are met in thee tonight…"

Ruth dropped her cigarette end to the ground and trod on it. "I imagine you don't want to go back in. It's a bit cold for you to wait around here for Mum and me. Are you okay to get home by yourself, if I wait for her?"

"Yes, I'm okay." Embarrassment made him mutter. "I'm really sorry to have ruined your evening."

"You haven't ruined it, but it's very sad to see someone so upset."

"It'll all be the same in a thousand years. Isn't that what they say? Your oid yew tree over there has probably seen a lot worse."

"Could be."

"Thank you for bringing my hat and coat."

"I thought you must be ill." She paused. "The play wasn't really that bad, was it?"

It was a clumsy attempt at humour, but Duncan was grateful for it. "I'll go home and put the kettle on," he said. "Go and look after your mother."

"You're sure you're all right?"

"Yes, and –"

"Don't keep saying you're sorry. Go home."

When the two women got back later, it soon became clear that Ruth had concocted a cover story to explain Duncan's rapid exit from the church. She had told her mother that he had experienced a sudden, very painful attack of cramp. It was probably due to the coldness of the church, and the fact that there was not much room in the pew, she said. To Duncan it seemed a weak story, but Mrs Cole accepted it, and treated the incident lightly in consequence. He was glad he did not have to produce an explanation of his behaviour. He was not entirely sure he could explain it even to himself. It was, he concluded, one of those sudden and increasingly rare moments of grief, grief which could never fully be expunged from his experience.

He wasted little time in going to bed. He was thoroughly exhausted. He almost dreaded going to sleep in case he dreamed of Audrey. He had begun to imagine that, after four years, the memories were now less vivid. It was a shock to find that was not true.

XV

Wednesday was Christmas Eve, a working day. Graham was glad not to have to spend it with Ruth and her mother. They planned to catch the bus into Hazlehurst to do some last-minute shopping. Apart from asking him if he felt any better Mrs Cole did not refer to the previous evening. She had accepted the explanation that Ruth offered.

It was obvious that she was taking great pleasure at having her daughter at home again for the week. Ruth chatted, mainly with her mother, about the proposed shopping trip, but Duncan was conscious of occasional, covert glances as she tried to judge how he really felt. He left them with the washing up and escaped.

He surprised young Jenny, handing her an envelope with two pound notes in it, and telling her she could have the rest of the day off. She stammered her thanks and left. He made a half-hearted attempt to occupy himself, checking invoices, but he could not concentrate. He sat inside and watched out for customers. He remained in a curiously disturbed state and, unbidden, images of his wife kept recurring, and he could not stop the words coming back, time and again in Audrey's voice, "And love will last, though we may die"... Each time, he had to make a conscious effort to suppress the stab of pain. Whatever he did, he could not rid himself of the strange mixture of misery and uncertainty, and he found his hands shaking when he lit a cigarette.

He made himself another cup of tea. As he returned to his desk, he saw the diminutive figure of Percy Champion, hands in pockets, heading slowly towards him. The boy reached the door, which stood open, and hesitated. "Can I come in?" he asked. Duncan nodded.

"Cup of tea?" he offered.

"Okay, ta."

"What are you doing out and about today? Don't you know it's Christmas? I thought you'd be at home with your parents."

"Just Mum. Dad's away again."

"At Christmas? Must be an important job."

Percy didn't reply, he just shrugged.

"I went to the carol service last night," said Duncan. "There were a lot of the children from the school there. I don't remember seeing you though."

"Nah. We never go."

"Well, you don't see me in church very often either."

Percy finished his tea and took the empty mug, together with Duncan's, over to the sink and rinsed them both. Duncan watched, secretly approving the boy; he wasn't really all bad, he told himself. He remembered he had used his sweet ration coupons on a bar of chocolate which was still in the desk. He took it out, broke off two squares, and gave them to the boy.

"So, it's just you and your mum for Christmas, is it?"

"Suppose so."

"Well," Duncan said, "I'm glad you dropped in. You've been pretty helpful over the past few weeks." It was not entirely true, but he wanted to cheer the boy up a little. "I owe you some wages."

"Wages?" Percy was taken aback.

Duncan opened the cash box and took out a one-pound note. "Buy yourself something," he said. For a moment Percy stood and looked at the note in his hand, hardly believing it. Then he said, "Cor, thanks Mr Frome."

Duncan grinned. "No, thank you."

He watched Percy as he walked back towards the road, looking composed, but, once he had reached the road, he was unable to restrain himself, and he broke into a run. Duncan grinned broadly as he saw the boy taking great leaps every few paces.

The interruption had been welcome. Now he was able to concentrate a little better on work. Two customers came to buy paraffin. One car called in for petrol. He took the money and the coupons and returned to the invoices. He was still busy with them when he realized someone else was coming across the forecourt on a bicycle. It was Graham Dampier.

"I gather you came to the carol service last night after all," he said. "I'm sorry I didn't see you or get the chance to say hello. In fact, I'm ashamed to say I wouldn't have known you were there, if it wasn't that Brenda told me. She also said you left early. She thought you might be ill."

"Nothing too serious," Duncan continued with the story invented by Ruth. " I couldn't sit still any longer. I thought it probably better not to go back in, in case it happened again."

"I'm glad it's nothing more serious. What a pity, though, that on your first visit you had to leave early. It's always a happy occasion, one of the few times in the year when the church is full. Everybody seems to enjoy singing carols, and the children make it special."

"Yes, it all seemed very – I was going to say jolly."

Graham laughed. "Yes, jolly is a good word. Christmas is always a good time. I suppose, if I'm honest, I prefer Easter. That's really the most important of all the Christian festivals."

"Don't push your luck," Duncan smiled back at him. "You won't find me attending an Easter service."

"Worth a try," Graham smiled back. "Happy Christmas to you. It was good to see Ruth Cole back in the village. She's a very nice young woman. It's a pity she decided to move away. I expect her mother is very glad to have her home."

"Yes, she is, and I imagine we shall have a very pleasant little Christmas together."

The Vicar got back on his bike and rode off. Duncan locked the door and walked across the road to the pub for a pint of beer and a ham sandwich. The bar was empty except for three or four old men, regular customers. They looked up long enough to see who had come in, but no one spoke. Duncan had learned in the first few days and weeks, that it would take time to be fully accepted. He was still an outsider, not to be trusted until he proved himself by the length of time he stayed. George passed the time of day. Duncan ate up, drank up and decided to lock up for the rest of the day. With the two women out shopping he could have the house to himself.

They got back late in the afternoon, as the light was fading. They had enjoyed their day out and were chatting animatedly. Mrs Cole said she would like to attend Midnight Mass, even though it was only twenty-four hours since the carol service. Ruth volunteered to go with her. Duncan was happy to bid them good night, when they left at eleven o'clock, and to go on to bed. Before he turned off the bedside light, he took a photograph album from the bottom of the wardrobe, and he sat in bed, looking at the black and white images. His emotions were under better control now. He could remember when and where each picture was taken but, unlike the previous night, they did not provoke a jolt to his heart. He felt sadness but it was lightened by remembered pleasure. He closed the album, turned off the light and slid down into the bed. He did not hear the women return.

On Christmas Day Mrs Cole was busy in the kitchen for most of the morning. Lunch would be at about 1 o'clock, and after lunch, when the table had been cleared and the dishes washed, they exchanged presents. Once the washing-up was done, before she set to work in the kitchen, Mrs Cole telephoned her daughter in Coventry. Duncan, sitting with a cigarette, could hear the conversation through the open door. Ruth shared the call with her mother. They both sounded very excited. They came back into the room smiling broadly. Ruth announced, "I'm going to be an auntie."

Duncan congratulated them. Ruth, who had noted her mother's expression, when she looked at Duncan, gave him a slightly puzzled look, but she was delighted at the news. She told her mother she had better start knitting matinee jackets and booties. There was much laughter and light spirits, very fitting for the occasion in this crowded, little room, festooned with paper decorations, sprigs of holly, ivy and a small bunch of mistletoe. Duncan had not realized he was standing underneath it until, still full of good cheer, Ruth took two small steps towards him, pointed upwards and gave him a quick kiss on the cheek. He was a little embarrassed but laughed it off.

He and Ruth trudged down the garden path to feed the chickens and to collect the eggs. It was very quiet outside. The air was cold. They were in no great hurry to go back inside, and stood in friendly silence, staring out at the view of the old elm trees, and the Downs beyond.

"Glad to be home?"

Ruth did not reply immediately. "I'd be lying if I said I didn't miss this," she admitted. "And there are times when it's nice to be completely quiet like this, without the traffic, and no boss telling you what to do."

"But you still don't want to come back."

"Not permanently, no."

"Well," Duncan said, "For my part I can't say I miss the town. I haven't really explored much of the countryside yet."

"I think tomorrow it would do us both good to go for a long walk. We shall probably spend the rest of today eating far too much. It's part of our tradition to have a couple of drinks too."

"I don't think I've ever seen your mother drink alcohol."

Ruth chuckled. "Christmas and New Year only," she said. "She won't want to do anything much tomorrow, and we usually have something like cold chicken for lunch. As for me, I think I feel like going for a tramp in the woods."

"I'd better come with you, in case he fights back."

"You'd be welcome," Ruth said with a laugh, "if you can stand the pace, that is."

"Cheeky!" Duncan reproved her.

"It'll be about four or five miles."

"Sounds good to me."

The rest of Christmas Day passed much as predicted. As Ruth had warned him, there was sparkling wine to accompany the food, and brandy to follow it. They were all uncomfortably full as Ruth and Duncan washed up the dishes and joined Mrs Cole in the sitting room. The fire blazed, making the room rather too hot, and Duncan found it hard to keep his eyes open as the hands of the clock neared 3 pm. They listened to the King's Speech in respectful silence, before Mrs Cole turned off the wireless, and they exchanged presents.

By 10 o'clock they were all drowsy from the food, the drink and the heat of the sitting room, and Duncan bade the two women good night and went to bed. As he put on his pyjamas, he realized with a sudden guilty start, that at no point during the day had thoughts of Audrey crossed his mind.

XVII

"I think it must have been something I ate," said Mrs Cole on Boxing Day morning. "I've got a bit of a headache this morning. I don't think I want to do very much. You won't mind if we only have something light to eat later, will you?"

Ruth and Duncan exchanged looks and smiled.

"If it's okay with you, Mum," Ruth said, "we'll get out of your hair and go for a walk. Duncan tells me he hasn't properly explored around here yet."

"Good idea. The fresh air will probably do you both good. To tell you the truth, I still feel quite tired. I might even go and lie down for an hour to shake off this headache. I think I'll take a couple of aspirin tablets."

This time, as well as a flask of tea, Duncan had a packet of sandwiches in the rucksack he carried. Ruth took him along the village street and turned down a track which led eastward down a little meadow to the stream close to the bottom of the churchyard. A farm track continued to the east, towards Belham, with the stream on their left. On the right-hand side of the track were hawthorn hedges and, beyond them, flinty, fallow fields. At the far side of the fields there was a hedge and scrubland at the bottom of the scarp side of the Down.

There was a gap leading into the first field, but no gate. There was a pungent smell of manure. Just inside the opening and to the left a huge dung heap steamed gently.

"Now, that is something I imagine you don't miss," said Duncan.

"Funnily enough, I do, in a way. There's nothing that reminds me more of the countryside than the smell of rotting manure."

"I think I'd prefer exhaust fumes."

"There speaks the mechanic."

"Didn't you say you learned a bit about car maintenance yourself?"

"Yes, a bit. I'd like to know more."

They walked on down the rutted lane. To their left the little stream was clear and bright, fringed with short plants. After half a mile the brook turned left, away from the track.

Now they were walking between smaller fields. The soil here was different, sandy rather than chalky, and the track divided, one branch leading off to the left.

"That's the track to the Frosts' place," Ruth said.

"Dorothy Frost and her son?"

"Dorothy doesn't have a son. She is not married."

"She may not be married," said Duncan, "but she certainly has a son. His name is Jack."

This was a real surprise. Ruth stopped.

"This is really good gossip," she said. "I don't remember Mum telling me about this. Are you sure?"

"Absolutely."

They walked on, following the right hand track until it came to an end at a five-barred gate. Attached to the gate was a faded wooden notice, "Private Keep Out. Trespassers will be Prosecuted – or Shot!"

"Don't worry," said Ruth, not bothering to open the gate. She climbed over and jumped down on the other side. "Come on. The wood is private, and usually we might be taking a chance, but not today."

"What's special about today?"

"The local hunt meets on Boxing Day in Hazlehurst. The gamekeeper has to be there. He is normally a bit - aggressive."

"Poachers? Is that why it says we could be shot?"

Ruth nodded. "That, and later in the year he rears the pheasants here. He's a nasty man."

"Because he shoots trespassers?"

"No." Ruth was very serious. She thought for a moment, then, "I remember him from when I was a little girl," she said. "He had a terrible reputation even then. Several of my school friends told me he had – behaved inappropriately, I think that's the way people put it."

"That's disgusting, if it's true."

"It's true, all right," she said, "we were all afraid of him."

"Didn't anyone report him?"

"We were only children. No one would have believed us."

"He could still be at it!"

"Yes. He didn't confine himself to children, either. There were rumours…Well, let's say several women had been propositioned, definitely, but there were two rapes that I heard about later. No one would report them. They didn't think anyone would believe them, and, well, it's very hard for a woman to accuse a man of rape. There aren't that many women police officers."

The revelations shocked Duncan to the core. They walked on in silence.

Before they entered The Chase, Duncan noticed that the wood extended towards the Downs and up the slope for some distance. They now turned in that direction. It was mixed woodland with occasional oaks, one or two majestic elms, ash trees, others that Ruth described as wild cherry, holly bushes and a few clumps of hazel. The trees were crowded together, and Duncan felt uneasy, almost a sense of eeriness.

Some fifty yards into the wood they came across a clearing. At this time of the year there was very little growing, although there was a scattering of dead undergrowth. In the middle there were large pens, a wooden framework covered in chicken wire. There were also some large, low, hut-like structures in which the birds could shelter. When Ruth explained their purpose, Duncan was puzzled that so much trouble was taken to rear thousands of little birds and protect them from foxes and other predators, only to shoot them when they were larger.

"The guns pay a lot of money for a shoot," Ruth explained.

At one side of the clearing there was a patch of ground which looked to Duncan's unpractised eyes different. He pointed it out to Ruth.

"It looks as though it's been dug over recently," she said. "Reuben White probably buried something he shot, but it must have been something he couldn't eat, a fox, maybe."

Soon the ground began to slope upwards, and they didn't talk any more than necessary. Towards the top of the hill there was another area composed largely of beech trees. The leaves inhibited other plants at ground level, so the view was of a large number of clean-limbed trees rising out of a reddish-brown carpet. Soon they came across the footpath which led further upwards and bore right. It was time for a break; they found a fallen tree to sit on. Duncan took the flask of tea from the rucksack and poured it into two cups. They sat for a little while in silence and smoked. There was little noise except for birdsong.

"Ruth," he said tentatively, "I think I owe you an explanation for my behaviour on Tuesday night."

She looked at him sharply. "It's none of my business," she said.

"That's exactly what your mother said."

"Mum?"

"Soon after I moved in, she spotted there was something wrong. When I said I wanted to explain, she said simply what you did, that it was none of her business."

"Well, it isn't."

Duncan did not know why he felt it so important to explain matters. He didn't really know Ruth that well, and in two days' time she would be returning to Luton. It would be a long time before he saw her again, if he ever did.

"It was the poem," he said, " It brought back a memory of my wife."

"Your wife!" It was difficult to understand Ruth's reaction from the tone of her voice. She was more than surprised – shocked perhaps? Certainly, she had been shaken. She stood up and took two or three paces away from the log. Then she turned towards him and said, as though she did not believe him, almost accusing him, "You are married?"

"No – yes – no," he said, momentarily tongue-tied. "Widowed. My wife's dead."

"Dead?"

"A German bomb." Even as he spoke, Duncan realized the words no longer upset him as they had in the past. It was as though he was making a report, stating a historical fact. Something had changed. He was at least as much concerned with Ruth's reaction as in the past, he would have been with the deep feelings of regret and anger at the information itself.

Ruth stood and stared at him. "No wonder you were so upset," she said. "When did this happen?"

"Just over four years ago."

"Is that why you moved down here?"

He nodded.

"I think I could do with another cigarette." She took one from him and sat down again. The mood had changed. Duncan was unsure if telling her had been the right thing to do.

Conversation dried up. Anything they said would be trivial. Better not to speak at all. Duncan repacked the rucksack and put it on his back. They resumed their walk through the tall trees and emerged on the open Down.

Mrs Cole sensed a change in the way they behaved towards one another, but she knew better than to ask the reason. The two young people were polite and talked casually enough, Ruth explaining the route they had taken, but there was something missing. There had been a mildly bantering tone between them until now, and that had gone. She had allowed herself the occasional flight of fancy, thinking maybe they might be romantically attracted, but there was certainly no evidence of that. Duncan seemed almost anxious in his manner. Well, she told herself, whatever this was about, it was their business, not hers, and, provided they had not developed a mutual dislike, they would survive until Ruth's departure on Monday.

XVIII

Mrs Cole was gratified, and Duncan surprised when Ruth gave him a quick hug and another kiss on the cheek as she said goodbye. His feelings towards her were confused. Ruth was direct and seemingly uncomplicated. He had been able to talk to her, and she to him about matters of deep concern. He remained unsettled and uneasy about her revelations on the subject of the gamekeeper. If there was any substance to the allegations she had made, then justice had not been done as yet. Rumours of rape were certainly awful to contemplate, but Duncan was also deeply disturbed by Ruth's talk of Reuben White's interfering with young girls.

His first, unpleasant encounter with Joe Champion, Percy's father, occurred several weeks later. He was working in the Old Forge. He stopped for a cup of tea, then realized that he had run out of cigarettes. He cleaned his hands as best he could and walked round the corner to the post office. As he turned to leave, he saw a man get out of a smart, black car. He was heading for the post office, but, before he could walk around the car, Gwen Proctor, the village school mistress, who was heading the same way from the school, called to him.

"Mr Champion!" she called. "You haven't replied to my letters!"

The man turned towards her, "What letters?"

"I've written to you twice, as I'm sure you will remember. I wanted you to come to see me to talk about Percy."

"What for?"

"His behaviour is becoming quite unacceptable. He's rude, not just to me, but to the other children. He needs discipline."

"Then discipline him. That's your job. Don't ask me to do it for you. He doesn't give me any lip, I can tell you, or I'd soon give him a slap, and he knows it."

"It's not that simple."

"Yes, it is, you stupid cow. Just do your job."

"Really! There's no need to be so rude!"

"You don't seem to understand anything else, or are you just bloody thick?"

At this, Duncan felt the need to intervene. "Don't talk to a lady like that!" he said, from the steps of the post office.

Joe Champion turned to face him. "Who the hell are you?" he asked.

"My name is Frome."

"Oh, you're the silly bugger that mends bikes for a living."

"Watch your language," Duncan said, "there are ladies present."

At this, Joe Champion laughed. "What ladies?"

"Percy must get his bad habits from you. If you don't respect his teacher, he won't."

"Mind your own bloody business. Who do you think you are? If you don't like it here, go back where you came from, and good riddance!"

Duncan restrained himself. His hands had already clenched, but he did not want to become involved in an undignified and pointless brawl. He walked away.

He was put out, a couple of days later, when he was accosted in his turn by Miss Proctor. "Mr Frome," she said, "I realize you were only trying to help, but I would be grateful if, in future, you did not interfere in my concerns. I am perfectly capable of dealing with parents like Mr Champion on my own."

"I'm sorry you take it that way," he said. "As you said, I was only trying to help. I rather like Percy."

"I suppose it's a good thing that someone can find good in him," she said. "He is really a quite objectionable child. He is uncooperative, slow to learn – he doesn't seem to want to learn anything – and he is disruptive, so he prevents the rest of the children from getting on as they should."

"Right! Perhaps he would benefit from a more sympathetic approach."

"I've been doing this job for many years," said Miss Proctor. "I think I know what I'm doing better than a mere casual observer."

Well, Duncan said to himself, as she walked away, with her head held arrogantly high, no wonder I've seen Percy playing truant. With a father who is hardly ever at home, and a teacher who makes no secret of her dislike for him, it isn't surprising the boy has no interest in learning. Yet, in the short time he had known Percy, Duncan recognised the boy not only had spirit, he also had enough natural curiosity to want to learn. He had begun to pick up quite a lot of knowledge from watching Duncan at work.

Joe Champion, now, he appeared to be a thoroughly unpleasant type. He wondered what kind of work took him to Brighton so much of his time. Whatever it was, it must pay well, because the car he had was in good condition by the look of it. Brighton wasn't that far away. It would take him no more than an hour to drive home. Perhaps the job required him to work unsocial hours. If it didn't, he could surely come home more frequently than every five or six weeks. He had, Duncan remembered, been away over Christmas. He had also heard it rumoured that Joe had been known to knock his wife about.

Duncan heaved a sigh; whatever the ins and outs of it, Percy's home life was not likely to provide him with a good start. Joe Champion, according to his son, had been a soldier. Maybe there were many like him, men who found it difficult to settle back into civvy street. The tightly controlled, disciplined life they had become used to made it difficult for some of them to live without the support of rules and regulations.

XIX

The New Year had come and gone. Duncan had seen nothing of Percy for several weeks, then he turned up one afternoon. Duncan was at his bench, where he was busy with a gearbox. His hands were covered in thick oil.

"Hello, Percy," he said, looking up, "long time, no see."

"Dad's gone back to Brighton," Percy explained. "He told me to stay away."

"Oh?"

"If it's OK with you, I'll still give you a hand when he's away."

"As you like," Duncan said. "You can help by going over to that bookshelf." Percy walked to the shelf, on which there was a row of manuals. "Find the one that has 'BSA Bantam' printed on the spine and bring it to me. Put it over there, where it's clean and I can see it, and open it at the section on 'Gears'."

But the boy made no attempt to do as he was asked.

"BSA Bantam," Duncan repeated.

Percy shook his head. "I can't read very well," he said.

"How old are you?"

"Ten, nearly."

"Well, you can't do anything, not even be a mechanic, unless you can read. Why haven't you learned at school?"

Percy shrugged. "Don't like school," he said.

Duncan cleaned his hands. "Well," he said, "at least make me a pot of tea."

They sat and drank tea out or enamel mugs, and ate biscuits.

"Percy," said Duncan, "I'll make a bargain with you: you come and help me but bring a reading book with you. You can only help me when you've read at least two pages."

It was said almost on the spur of the moment, but Duncan sensed there was potential in this young boy. Gwen Proctor, seemed to have given up on him. "Well," he said, "what do you say?"

"Two pages!"

"Let's see how much there is on a page."

The bargain was struck. Duncan solemnly spat in his palm, Percy did likewise, and they shook hands. So began the private tuition. Neither of them could foresee the consequences.

Duncan thought little of this, though he went through with his part of the bargain. Percy took to calling into the workshop after school most afternoons. When he did, Duncan was happy to take a break, share a mug of tea, and listen to the boy as he stumbled through a page of simple English. After a few weeks Percy was clearly improving. One reason, Duncan realized, was that no one previously had shown any real interest in him; even his teacher seemed ready to write the boy off as a waste of time.

It was inevitable that Miss Proctor noticed the improvement. She was surprised, and said so, but was inclined to think this was only a flash in the pan. Nevertheless, she felt obliged to acknowledge the improvement in Percy's reading, and mentioned it to Mrs Champion, whom she met by chance on one of her occasional visits to the village shop. Percy's mother, who lived in a dreary world of anxiety and depression, began to take more interest in her son's progress.

"Miss Proctor says you're doing much better," she said.

"Yeah, I suppose I am."

"Why is that, do you think?"

Percy, surprised by her sudden interest, told her how Mr Frome had been helping him. "He lets me help with the bikes and things," he said, "but only if I read to him."

"Well, that's very good of him," his mother said, "but you had better not say anything to your dad. You know what he's like."

"OK."

Mrs Champion took it upon herself one afternoon to visit Duncan. He had seen her once or twice in the village, but he had never spoken to her. She seemed to flit around like an animated shadow, as though seeking not just anonymity but invisibility. He was, therefore, very surprised when she walked in. He turned from his bench to greet her and ask her what he could do for her.

"Mr Frome?"

"Yes, that's me."

"I believe you've been helping my son, Percy, with his reading."

"Did he tell you that?"

"Yes, and he seems to have taken a sudden interest in learning to read. It must be down to you, I think."

"He's a good lad really," said Duncan. "He only wanted someone to show an interest."

"Well," she said, "I just wanted to say thank you."

Duncan acknowledged the thanks with a shrug of his shoulders. "Can I offer you a mug of tea?" he asked.

She shook her head, but Duncan sensed that she had not finished what she had come to say. He took out a cigarette and lit it, waiting for her to speak.

"This is awkward," she said. "It's very good of you to help Percy like this, but –."

"But?"

"You've never met my husband, Joe, have you?"

"Oh yes, we had, let's say a bit of a run-in some time ago."

"Ah! In that case you probably know he has a short fuse."

"I can't say I took to him, if I'm honest."

"No. He doesn't make many friends. The fact is, Joe has a bad temper: he can even be quite violent."

"What's that got to do with me?"

"If he gets to know that Percy has been coming to see you, especially when he's been told not to, I don't like to think what he might do."

"You think he might even punish the boy?"

"Yes. He believes in the saying 'Spare the rod and spoil the child'. I wouldn't put it past him to blame me, too. But that isn't why I wanted to talk to you, not really. Joe is bound to find out about this sooner or later, and, when he does, he will probably come after you, too."

"I can look after myself, I promise you, and it would be a shame to stop Percy coming to see me. His reading has improved in leaps and bounds. If I told him to stop coming, he might give up trying, and that would be a pity. In for a penny, in for a pound: it won't really matter whether he stops coming to me or not, I imagine Joe is likely to be angry either way."

"Well," Mrs Champion said, as though she despaired of her ability to persuade him, "don't say you haven't been warned."

She turned abruptly and slipped out, walked quickly across the forecourt, and hurried into the shelter of the footpath that led underneath the row of horse-chestnut trees in the recreation ground next door. Duncan returned to his bench, his mind busy with sad thoughts about this small, dysfunctional family. When Percy called in later, he made him read longer than usual.

XX

One afternoon Duncan left young Jenny to look after the petrol pump and returned home early. It was half term, so Percy would not be calling. He had received a letter from Ruth, a friendly letter, written in the same kind of open, mildly amusing style. He was not a great letter writer himself, but he wanted to reply. However, he was very surprised to find Mrs Cole sitting at the kitchen table on which she had spread newspaper. She was busy cleaning a shotgun.

"It was my husband's," she explained. "I often used to clean it for him. He used it to shoot rabbits for the pot."

"That's a dangerous thing to have lying around."

"Oh, I usually keep it locked away. "

"So, why have you got it out now?"

"You probably haven't noticed, but there are a few rats at the end of the garden. They'll be after the eggs. I thought I'd have a go myself, see if I can get a few of them."

"Sounds a bit dangerous to me." Duncan was concerned at the thought of this small and elderly woman using a lethal weapon. "Doesn't your dog get them for you?"

"Not a chance. He's far too fat and lazy these days."

"I must say, Mrs Cole, I don't like the thought of you wondering around with a gun in your hand."

"Well, something has to be done. What about you? Would you like to have a go?"

It was not exactly something that Duncan would have thought of doing, but he was used to being round guns. He agreed. The gun was in good condition, it had been carefully looked after and oiled before it had been locked away. The barrel was clean and the trigger mechanism, including the safety catch, was in good repair. There were half a dozen cartridges in a box. He stuffed them in a pocket and took the gun to the end of the garden, beyond the chicken run. The old lady was right. He stood, not making a sound, as evening fell. After a while a large rat scurried along the edge of the rough grass where the chalky soil bordered the field. It stopped. Duncan slipped two cartridges into the breech and snapped it shut. The rat moved a few inches forward and stopped again, its whiskers quivering. He raised the gun and fired. He had forgotten how loud the sound was. The rat was dead.

He broke the gun and removed the unused cartridge, then he picked up the rat by its tail and took it as far as the kitchen door.

"Well done!" said Mrs Cole.

The farmer who owned the adjacent fields was happy for him to hunt rabbits. They were a real pest as well as a source of cheap food. Like rats, they bred rapidly, and Duncan did his best to reduce the population of both species.

XXI

Duncan, whose only experience with a gun previously had been with a Lee Enfield rifle during basic training, was surprised how easy it was to obtain a gun licence. Unless you were certified insane, or had a criminal record, it was simple. He was not over-enthusiastic about it, but he did not want Mrs Cole to risk using a firearm. She laughed at his worries on that score. She wasn't senile yet, she told him.

He needed to buy new cartridges. The shop was in Hazlehurst. Mrs Cole gave him directions. It was a small shop on one of the few side-streets, a combined gunsmith's and saddler's. Duncan, unfamiliar with all the leatherwork and tack, looked in the shop window and recognised the craftsmanship. He was coming to realize there were many aspects of country life that were new to him, a townee. No doubt all this leatherwork was an integral part of the fox-hunting scene. He went in.

There was only one man serving, a short man in his sixties, very quick and efficient. He was dealing with a swarthy man, strongly built, who said little. The shopkeeper had just collected a large box which, according to the label, contained six dozen shot-gun cartridges. He put them on the counter. Duncan saw that a name had been written in big letters on the box, Reuben White. So, this was the "aggressive game-keeper" that Ruth had spoken of.

"Put them on the Estate account," he said, and picked them up. Duncan was obliged to squeeze against the wall so he could get to the door but, instead of thanking him, Reuben White said, "Mind your bloody self, will you?"

Duncan raised his eyebrows as he turned to the shopkeeper.

"Don't take it personally," said the man, as the bell tinkled and the door closed, "Reuben White's always like that, not too well-endowed in the manners department."

"Is that the gamekeeper?"

The shopkeeper nodded. "He works for the Estate, though I don't know what work he's been doing these past few years, not rearing pheasants, that's sure enough. I imagine it's starting up again now the war's over. What can I do for you, sir?"

Duncan made his modest purchase and left.

The High Street in Hazlehurst was unusually wide. On either side of the tarmac road there was another strip of cobbles, the same width as a traffic lane. These were available for parking, and Duncan had left his motorbike and sidecar halfway down the street, facing back towards Hartsfoot. As he stowed his heavy parcel in the sidecar, he noticed the mud-splattered van on the other side. It was a five-hundredweight van which was filthy, but there was enough paint showing to see that it was green, the same colour as could be seen on all the Estate properties. On the side of the van Duncan could read Consolidated Investments. So, the Estate was not in one person's ownership, but belong to a syndicate.

From his left another vehicle approached. This one was a pickup truck and, by the sound of it, in need of care and attention. The exhaust was clearly blown, and that might be one of the reasons that the engine seemed to be running very raggedly. It pulled onto the cobbles behind the green van and stopped. The driver was a young lad. In the passenger seat was a face that Duncan had seen before, and he now recognised as

Dorothy Frost. This must be her son, Jack. The pair were in great spirits. Whatever they had been talking about, they were now laughing happily as Dorothy walked round to the driver's side. At that moment the large figure of Reuben White emerged from the newsagent's on Duncan's right, and walked purposefully across the road. He was carrying the parcel of cartridges, which must have weighed a great deal, as though it contained feathers. He appeared not to notice the mother and son, but he opened the rear doors of his van and stowed the parcel away. He slammed the door shut with a clang and walked round to the driver's door, climbed in, and made off, leaving a small cloud of exhaust fumes.

Duncan would have thought nothing of this as, in his turn, he walked round to the offside of his combination, but, as he was about to take his seat, he heard Jack's voice.

"Are you all right, mum?" He sounded anxious. Duncan looked up. Where, a moment ago, Dorothy Frost had been laughing merrily with her son, she now looked quite ill. She had lost all colour from her face, and she was leaning against the side of the pickup, as though afraid she might fall. Duncan took a few quick steps across the road, but Dorothy was already saying, "I'm all right. Don't make a fuss. I've just had a funny turn, that's all. Give me a minute. You go and do the shopping. I'll sit inside for a moment and wait for you."

Duncan said, "Mrs Frost, I'm Duncan Frome, the one with the workshop. You don't look at all well, and I think your son is right to be worried. Maybe you should see a doctor."

"I'm all right!" She was impatient, cross perhaps, that she had drawn attention to herself in this way. "It's just a funny turn. I'll be all right in a moment."

"Well," said Duncan, "let me at least buy you a cup of tea." The little teashop was only a few yards away from where they were parked. "I'm not taking no for an answer."

Dorothy made as if to refuse, but then gave in as though the effort was too much. She refused to take his arm, nevertheless, and walked a little unsteadily to the café, where they sat at a table near the window and Duncan ordered tea and cakes, while Jack, seeing his mother safely installed, decided the best bet would be for him to do the shopping on his own. They didn't need very much, and it would give his mother time to recover.

Duncan did not ask any questions. He made small talk, and he was relieved to see the colour coming back into her cheeks, but he was still a little anxious. Whatever had caused this "turn", it had looked alarmingly like a stroke. He knew nothing about the Frosts, although he had inevitably been at least partially briefed by Martha. Martha, he had quickly recognised, was keenly interested in every piece of gossip that came her way, or which she could unearth.

"That motor of yours sounds pretty dreadful, if you don't mind my saying so," he said.

There was the faintest smile of acknowledgement. "Yes, I know," she said. "We really should get it done, but I can't really do without it, and it's such a hassle, and with the driving all the way here, catch a bus back, wait three days, and then come back by bus to pick it up."

"I'll have a look at it, if you like."

"Well…"

"I wouldn't charge you the earth, and I am a qualified mechanic."

"I'd still have to get the bus back."

"Why don't you get your son to bring it down to me? I could bring him back, and then I could come and collect him when it's done."

Dorothy thought for a moment. "I wouldn't want to put you out," she said.

"It wouldn't be any trouble. The sooner you get that exhaust fixed, the better. I don't know if you realize it, but the engine doesn't work as well. When did you last have it serviced?"

Dorothy made a face at this, as though embarrassed by the question. "It hasn't been properly serviced for about two years," she said. "I've changed the oil and the spark plugs, and I've even checked the brakes. I'm not totally incapable, Mr Frome, I've even been known to work on my old Fordson."

"A tractor?"

"A very old tractor. It's still going, that's the main thing."

By now she was looking much better. When Duncan asked for the bill, she wanted to pay, and he had to argue quite strenuously. Jack appeared as they were leaving the café. The anxiety on his face disappeared when he realized that his mother was back to her normal self. Briskly, she explained Duncan's offer, and the matter was decided there and then. Duncan left them to make their own, noisy way home, and he walked across to his motorcycle, started with one quick stamp of his foot, raised a hand in farewell, and headed homeward.

It would be a long time before the significance of this little episode became clear. For the time being, he simply assumed that Dorothy had been overcome by a fainting fit, and he did not think too much about it. Jack, however, was not so quick to dismiss it. He suspected that his mother might be concealing a serious illness. He did not want to upset her further by repeated mention of her "funny turn", but he would not be satisfied until he got to the bottom of it. When he did, at last, understand, the consequences would be grave.

XXII

At the beginning of July the countryside was at its best after the coldest winter in living memory, and the weather was dry. Mervyn Hardcastle, the genial old man on the Parish Council, approved of Duncan's enterprise. After one meeting he invited him to his house for a chat. Duncan was not at all sure why, but he duly walked up to the house one evening. It was about fifty yards along the lane past the pub. The banks here rose about eight feet from the road. Access to each of these large houses was by a flight of steps. Duncan found a name plate at the bottom of the second set of steps, opened the gate at the top, underneath the heavy greenery of sycamores in full leaf, and found himself on a large, circular gravel driveway. Moto access was at the other side. Here there was a beautiful lawn which he walked across, but he felt as though he was committing an act of desecration. The house was of brick and, apart from its size, unpretentious. He found the door and rang the bell.

Mervyn led him through a hallway. The parquet floor gleamed. They entered a drawing room. It all seemed luxurious to Duncan's eyes: there were two large, leather sofas either side of a long coffee table. On the walls there were pictures and framed examples of Chinese calligraphy. Once Duncan was seated, Mervyn plunged straight in.

"You already realize that I approve of your enterprise," he said. "So, I hope you will not be offended at what I have to say."

Duncan wondered what was coming.

"Of course, I have no idea of your financial state," Mervyn continued, "but I imagine you will be finding it quite difficult and expensive to start a new business, especially at this time, when money is tight."

"It is expensive, that's true, but I'm managing quite nicely, thank you. It's a matter of staying patient. I have to establish myself and set up a proper customer base. That takes time."

Mervyn nodded. "Yes, I had imagined that you would have a long-term plan. But I'll come to the point. Since I made this village my home, I have been keen to see it improve and prosper. I imagine that an injection of capital at this point would help you to speed up your plans. I've had a lot of experience in business and I have carried out plenty of negotiations with banks in the past. If you can provide a viable business plan, I would be prepared to invest…"

Duncan was startled and he showed it. He opened his mouth to speak but Mervyn held up his hand. "Don't be alarmed," he said, "this is not an attempt to take you over. I would not want to play an active part in any way. I would draw up a legal agreement with you and lend you – let's say £5000 – at commercial rates, less than a bank would charge. In return I would expect shares in your business, say twenty per cent. It would, of course, all depend on the quality of your business plan. What do you say?"

Duncan was struck dumb for a moment. "I need to think about it," he said. "It sounds like a very generous offer. I'm not quite sure how you would want me to set out a business plan."

"I would be very alarmed if you had said yes immediately. Of course, you will need to think about it, and of course we would need to talk about it at some length. If you decide you are in any way interested, the business plan becomes crucial, and I would get my accountant to check it through before any such agreement was signed. For you this could mean an opportunity to develop the business much more rapidly than otherwise."

"I'll think about it," Duncan said.

"Let me at least offer you a drink. Tea? Coffee? Something stronger?"

He opted for tea. Mervyn left the room for a moment, then came back and settled into his place again. Perhaps he had forgotten already. He began asking a few questions about the workshop, the repairs, the amount of work that was coming in. Duncan began to answer, but there was a tap on the door, then the housekeeper came in with a little trolley, laid with cups, saucers and tea plates, complete with a Victoria sponge cake. She served the two men and withdrew.

Duncan was not entirely comfortable in this environment. He was not used to being waited on, nor to being surrounded by such a show of wealth. He stayed a little longer to be polite, then left the way he had come.

Mervyn's offer occupied his thoughts for the next few days. If he were to accept the loan, he was afraid it would be like giving up part of the control of his own business. On the other hand, a sizeable investment at this point would enable him to advertise, buy some much-needed equipment, maybe, if the demand was there, take on apprentice. If the loan was to be subject to a proper, legal contract, scrutinised by a solicitor and even by an accountant, maybe he could ensure that the terms suited him. A few days later he made up his mind and phoned Mervyn Hardcastle. He was, he said, interested in the idea. Mervyn expressed satisfaction rather than excitement, and said he would set the wheels in motion.

XXIII

Percy's visits stopped suddenly, a sure sign that his father was back. Duncan had got used to the daily visits, when for a short time he assumed the role of schoolteacher-cum-parent. Three days after Percy's last visit, Duncan was reorganising the bicycles in his large wooden shed. He had taken three of them outside and leaned them against the wall, when he had men's voices coming from the direction of the Coach and Horses. He turned to see Joe Champion marching towards him. Two other men were following him, a few steps behind, as though he had set off quickly and surprised them.

"Don't, Joe!" one of the men shouted after him. Joe took no notice but marched up to Duncan and stopped so close to him that he could smell the beer on his breath.

"I told you once before to mind your own bloody business," he said loudly. He was clearly in a mood for a fight.

"What are you talking about now?" Duncan remained calm. Every time he saw this man he disliked him more.

"I'll have you for enticement," Joe said. "I told you to stay away from my boy, but you've been encouraging him into this dump. Well, he won't be coming back again, I can promise you that."

"What have you done?" Duncan was alarmed.

"None of your business. He won't be disobeying me again for some time, though, and I don't think he will want to sit down for a bit either."

"You've been bullying him? What kind of father are you?"

"Well, at least I do have children. Don't suppose you're able to, are you?"

Duncan's gorge rose at this, and to restrain himself he turned away. It was the wrong thing to do. Joe grabbed him by the shoulder, swung him round, and punched him hard on his right cheek. Taken by surprise, he staggered, tripped and fell. He was just in time to see Joe's booted foot swing towards his head. He grabbed it with both hands, twisted and pulled. Joe fell heavily on his back, yelling obscenities. By now the two men who had followed him arrived and grabbed an arm each. They pulled him forcibly away, almost frog-marching him. Over his shoulder, amid all the swear words, Joe was shouting, "And keep away from my missus! I know she's been coming here to see you. Keep away or next time…" The rest of the threat was inaudible as his two guardians took him back to the pub.

Duncan was shaken. It was a long time since he had come across such animosity. True, this little incident had been fuelled by drink, but Joe Champion had obviously developed more than just a dislike for him. His first impression of Joe had been that of a swaggering bully. Now he was very worried what he might have done to his son and to his wife. Duncan had heard the stories: while his wife, theoretically at least, had a choice, and could conceivably walk away for good, Percy had no option. He was the innocent victim of a father who seemed to be a thug.

By the time he got home after work he had a black eye. Mrs Cole, who showed her usual concern, was probably one of the last people in the village to know the story. Martha Brewer was quite cross that she only had of it second-hand. After all if it happened right on her doorstep. People muttered and shook their heads, but nothing much came of the fight: it didn't cross Duncan's mind to lay a complaint with the village bobby. For all he knew, he and Joe might be friends. They had both lived in the village longer than Duncan.

XXIV

Martha's bedroom was at the back of the house. Her bedroom window overlooked the Old Forge and Duncan's workplace. Unfortunately, there was a large pear tree in her garden and it completely blocked the view. She had at one time toyed with the idea of having the tree cut down, but it still produced fruit every year and she was quite fond of it. For at least half the year, at times when the moon was less than half full, it would not have been possible to see anything at night in any case. Conservation won the day and the tree remained.

Some four weeks after the fight between Duncan Frome and Joe Champion, Martha woke in the middle of the night the feeling that something was wrong. She looked at the luminous dial of her alarm clock. It said 2:30 AM. Her heart was beating rapidly. She sat up in bed and listened, half expecting to hear noises from downstairs. The house was silent, but she could hear something odd, a kind of crackling sound, and it was coming from outside. Gingerly she crept to the window, drew the curtains back and gave a little cry. Duncan's big wooden shed at the far side of the plot, was on fire. However the fire had started, it was now well ablaze, the flames leaping up the walls.

She pulled a dressing gown over her nightie and went downstairs to dial 999. Once she knew that the Fire Brigade was on its way from Hazlehurst, she covered her curlers with a headscarf, took a torch, and hurried outside to watch the spectacle. As she reached the point from which she had overheard the initial conversation between Duncan and George, the publican, the roof of the shed collapsed, throwing a cloud of smoke and sparks high into the air. Some landed in the adjacent sycamore trees, which were in full leaf and full of sap. There was the faintest of breezes, blowing the smoke away from the forecourt, and Martha suddenly realized how dangerous such a fire might have been, if the wind had been blowing in another direction. It was only a matter of yards to the petrol pump. The shed, she knew, was where Duncan stored not only his bicycles, but also his stock of paraffin. No wonder there was such heat coming from the fire that she could feel it in the road.

By the time the fire engine arrived there was nothing left of the shed or its contents other than the blackened skeletons of half a dozen bicycles and the remains of a very large wood fire. Martha made cups of tea for the firemen. She was far too excited to go back to bed and, although she was, as she said repeatedly, dreadfully tired for the rest of the day, she had something important to talk about to everybody. She phoned the news desk of the local paper and gave an eyewitness account. When she found her name in the following week's edition, she carefully cut out the report and stuck it in her treasured scrapbook.

The fire resulted in a small but perceptible change in the villagers' attitude towards Duncan. There was a short but marked pause in conversation when he entered the shop. Heads turned in unison when he approached a group of village women talking together. The charred remains of the hut were a reminder to those waiting for a bus at the bus stop outside the Coach and Horses. The suspicion he had perceived in the weeks immediately following his arrival now returned, and it was tinged with hostility. It was not a good atmosphere in which to grow his business.

He was glad that he had agreed in principle to take up Mervyn Hardcastle's offer. The shed and its contents were insured, but the disruption to his business was costly. With the additional investment he could survive the next few months as well as redevelop his business plan on a more ambitious scale. Officialdom was unhelpful: the senior fire officer was scathing in his comments about Duncan's constructing a wooden shed in which he stored paraffin, and to have done so in proximity to petrol storage tanks was, he said, madness, asking for a catastrophe to happen. He insisted that planning permission to rebuild should only be given for a building of brick or other, non-flammable material. He assumed that the fire had been caused by carelessness: arson was not even mentioned in his report. A similar line was taken by the insurance assessor. He was inclined at first to dismiss Duncan's protestations that there was nothing stored in the shed which might have started the fire, although it had to be admitted, once it had begun, it was unstoppable. Settlement of the claim took more than three months.

Mervyn Hardcastle was undeterred fortunately. Duncan took up his offer, found a local company to carry away the remains, and commissioned a builder to construct a combined office, storeroom and showroom. It took another three months to obtain the planning permission for this development. It was a stressful time.

Except for the sale of petrol and occasional jobs, minor repairs to motorcycles and sometimes cars, his time was largely taken up with paperwork, which he disliked intensely. His frustration and anger were vented to some degree by his new hobby, shooting rabbits. He saw them as vermin which had to be controlled.

With time on his hands, he also wrote letters to Ruth, who responded in the same, friendly tone. When she returned for his second Christmas in Hartsfoot, he was genuinely pleased to see her. By this time, he was feeling more optimistic, but impatient. The new building could begin as soon as the winter frosts permitted. He found a sympathetic listener in Ruth when he joined her once more for walks.

However, Ruth had her own worries. Her job, it seemed, was under threat. There was competition from men who had returned from the war, having learned to drive. Their needs, as wage earners and providers for families, tended to take precedence. She thought this was unfair; she was a skilled and very capable driver, but she was likely to be faced with the sack in a month or two.

Listening to her, Duncan began to formulate a plan. He said nothing to Ruth, but, if the worst came to the worst, and she had to return to Hartsfoot until another job became available, he might be able to help. The Old Forge was still functioning as a workshop, but, as well as the large, new building which would replace the burnt-out shed, one further facility was planned, an extension to the Forge itself, with an inspection pit. This would enable him to carry out work on cars, perhaps the occasional lorry. If his plans were successful, an apprentice would prove very helpful. Ruth had said that she would like to learn more about being a mechanic. Much would depend on his picking up business. There were a few more vehicles about now, and he had to remain optimistic. As for his relationship with the rest of the village, it would just take time.

XXV

A short time after this incident, Percy reappeared at the door of the Old Forge. "Can I come in?" he asked.

"I take it your dad is away again?"

"Yeah, good riddance!"

"You shouldn't say that about your own dad."

"What's he ever done for me?"

"He brought you into the world."

"Nah, that was mum. All he ever does is belt me one when he's had a drink. You've done more for me than he does."

Out of the mouths of babes and sucklings, Duncan thought. "You'd better come in," he said, "but I haven't got much work to do, not since the fire."

"Wotchyer going to do about it?"

"Are you really interested?"

"Yeah, course I am."

"Have you got your reading book with you?"

"No, I wasn't sure…"

"OK, I'll forgive you this time, but remember we had a deal, and I'll hold you to in future."

"You mean I can come back?"

"Why not?"

"I heard how my dad had a go at you."

"All the more reason, that's what I say."

Relationships re-established, they shared a pot of tea, and Duncan spread the plans on the bench and explained what the new building would look like, once all the planning was finished.

"Cor! It's going to look very posh!"

Duncan laughed. "I hope so," he said.

"It's going to cost a hell of a lot of money."

"You're right there." Duncan pulled a face. "Sometimes you have to spend money to make money."

The visits and the reading lessons resumed as before.

PART TWO

Enter The Bear

I

After morning milking, young John Stevens helped his father move the herd to the new pasture down the lane. John went ahead so that he could open the gate to the field, which was next to The Chase, the wood where Duncan and Ruth had taken their walk in the winter. The gate had not been opened for some time and John struggled at first, but he managed to drag it across the tangle of grass, effectively blocking the lane. The slow, lumbering cows could not be hurried, but they would automatically turn into the field when they encountered the barrier. As he leaned on it, he became aware of a dog, barking insistently. He looked round in the direction of the sound; it was coming from The Chase. That was peculiar. No one other than the gamekeeper ever went into the wood and, according to legend, Reuben White would have no compunction about shooting a stray animal, even a domestic pet, if it intruded into 'his' property. Leaving the gate, and risking his father's wrath, John investigated.

It was only a few yards to the gateway to The Chase, with its warning sign, badly faded but still legible. John did not need to go in; the dog, which continued to bark, was on the inside of the gate. It was a large, black dog. He spoke to it as soothingly as he knew how, but the barking continued as loudly as ever. The animal did not seem to be aggressive, however. When it saw John, it continued to bark urgently, but repeatedly turned back towards the wood, as though wanting him to follow. Mindful of the gamekeeper's reputation, John was reluctant. Instead, he stayed on the outside of the gate and shouted as loudly as he could, "Mr White! Are you there?" He waited a minute or two, then repeated his question. The dog continued to bark.

John looked back down the lane; the first two cows had already entered the pasture, the farmer was at the back of the other twenty-eight cows. John climbed over the gate into The Chase. As he had hoped, the dog did not approach him or threaten him, although he had a large stick in his hand, just in case. Instead, it turned, and took a few paces into the wood, stopped barking, and turned its head to check that John was following. His heart was beating loudly. He was scared that he might come face-to-face with the gamekeeper who, he knew, always appeared to carry a gun, certainly on the few occasions when John had seen him. The dog led him about a hundred yards into the trees, and stopped in the middle of a small clearing. In front of him John saw someone lying on the ground. He ran a few steps to where the dog was standing guard, and saw, with a shock, that there had been a serious accident: it looked as though the gamekeeper had managed to fire his shotgun in such a way as to shoot himself in the chest. The dog, now silent, was standing by the body of his master, and looking up at John, looking for help. There was nothing that the boy could do. He had seen dead animals, never a dead person, but he was pretty sure Reuben White was beyond anyone's help.

John reached out and stroked the dog's head. It allowed him to.

"You'd better come with me, boy," he said. "We've got to tell somebody about this."

He straightened up, but, as he turned to retrace his steps, something caught his eye, half-hidden in a thick growth of fireweed. He took four steps towards it and parted the weeds with his stick. He felt the hair on the back of his head stand up in horror: a second body, with a similar gunshot wound to its chest, lay, staring at the sky. John wheeled around and ran back to the entrance, clambered over the gate, and ran to find his father, who had closed off the field and was looking, worriedly in John's direction.

The dog had followed John, who now stammered out what he had seen. When, at last, Mr Stevens was able to make some sense of what he heard, he checked for himself, leaving John waiting in the lane. He came back, grim-faced, and the two returned to the farmhouse. Mr Stevens dialled 999. They drank tea and waited for the police. Reuben White's dog ate a plate of food.

II

Martha Brewer saw PC Trevor Mallow approaching on his bike. He stuck out his left hand as if to call in at the post office, but instead, he sailed past and turned sharp right down the lane that led to the brook. There was nothing else down there except, a good way down, the Frost farm. Maybe young Jack had been up to some mischief or other. Young men of that age often seemed to get into mischief. Dorothy Frost was an infrequent visitor, so it might be difficult to find out what was going on. Maybe, if she dropped a hint to Brenda Dampier, the Vicar's wife, she would get to find out in due course, but it was frustrating.

Her curiosity rose a couple of notches when, half-an-hour later, a Wolsey turned in from the opposite direction. The bell on the front told her immediately that it was a police car. It paused for a moment right in front of her door, and Martha could see the driver and the man next to him were both in police uniform. There were two other men in the back. In just a matter of seconds the car began moving again and it, too, turned down the lane which led to the Frost farm. A second car followed less than a minute later. Something serious must have happened. What could be so serious that it required two cars full of policemen? Martha's head was buzzing with speculation.

III

Inspector Edward Blundell, known by everybody in the Woodbury nick as "The Bear" (the connection, Edward – Ted – teddy bear, was obvious), was not especially intelligent. He had to work very hard to pass his Sergeant's examination, and even harder to secure promotion to Inspector rank. He was content with that, which was perhaps just as well, since further promotion would be highly unlikely. He had moved from the uniformed branch to CID almost by chance. When he was a Sergeant, he had been drawn into a case, when there was a severe shortage of available detectives. Almost by mistake he had succeeded in eliciting information from a reluctant witness, which led to a conviction. His interrogation methods were unorthodox, but proved remarkably effective, not only in this, his first case, but in several, successive cases. Not being one to beat about the bush, he treated every interview as an interrogation, an interrogation in which he assumed the person he was addressing was guilty, if not of the crime under investigation, then of something else. It was a tactic which worked frequently, because the witness or suspect was totally shocked, even outraged, and therefore thrown off-guard. He or he was then in a vulnerable, emotional state, and likely to say things which they would not normally admit. It was an extremely blunt instrument, but it often avoided the need for detailed, analytical detective work. To follow a logical train of thought made Bear's head ache.

At this precise moment he was bored. He was also fed up. There had been nothing much for the past three weeks but routine matters to occupy him. He could find no excuses to ignore the job of sorting out expenses claims and other paperwork. The and there was, as his colleagues and, more especially, his subordinates readily admitted, nothing worse than The Bear with a sore head.

The 999 call was anonymous. The telephonist said that the man sounded panicky. He had said someone had been killed in the woods in Hartsfoot, a wood called The Chase. The Bear was glad of the excuse to round out his small team, organised two cars and drive the 10 miles to the village. The Chase, which he had no trouble identifying on the map, was a little way to the east of the village, down a narrow lane which turned into a farm track. At the end of the track the car halted. This was obviously the right place, but the entrance to the wood was blocked by a large gate. They would have to walk from here, but The Bear was not prepared to climb over the locked gate.

"The damned thing is chained," he said. "I hope you got some bolt cutters in the boot." They had, and it took only a second to cut through the large padlock. It took the combined efforts of three men to force open the gate, which must have been closed for years. By the time they had gained access, another policeman arrived, breathless, on a bicycle.

"Are you the village constable?"

"Yes, sir, Constable Mallow."

"Good. You can come with me and tell me what you know."

"The first I heard about this, sir, was when I got a call this morning from Woodbury."

The Bear led the way into the trees. The wood was deserted. It was a strange place for death, a silent copse except for the birdsong all about them. When they arrived at the clearing, The Bear stopped. This was obviously the spot. The body of a man lay on its back.

"Oh my God!" The constable was shocked. He turned pale as he saw the bloodstains on the man's chest. Then he turned to one side suddenly, and was violently sick.

"Pull yourself together man!" The Bear was impatient. "Do you recognise this man?"

"Yes, sir, sorry, sir. It's the gamekeeper, Reuben White. He must have had an accident, shot himself."

"Is he a contortionist by any chance?" The Bear was sarcastic. "He seems to be lying on his gun. Tell me, constable, how did he manage to shoot himself in the chest, place the gun behind him and then fall on it?"

"No, I see what you mean, sir."

The Bear turned to his team and began the procedure of sealing off a large area around the scene of the incident. No one, he said, should disturb any part of the scene, certainly until the photographer had done his stuff. He alone stepped a little closer to the body, and, in doing so, he saw the second body, which had been hidden by the willow-herb. The second body had also been shot in the chest, apparently by a shot gun at close range. An arm's-length from the dead man, on his left, there was another shot gun.

This was something of a puzzle. Had they shot each other? How could that be? It could only be that way if the shots had been virtually simultaneous, but, in that case, how did the gamekeeper's gun come to be under his body? If the gamekeeper had shot an intruder, the intruder would have been in no condition to return the compliment and, in any case, the mystery of the position of the gamekeeper's gun remained.

Apart from securing the site, there was not much more they could do until the forensics had been done. Meanwhile, The Bear insisted on a careful search of the ground between the trees. While this was in progress he tried to find out as much as he could about both victims by talking to PC Mallow.

"Who is the other man? Do you know?"

"That's Joe Champion."

"And - ?"

"And what, sir?"

"What else do you know about him? What does he do? Where does he live? What's his relationship with the gamekeeper here?"

PC Mallow found it difficult to answer three questions at once. The Bear suspected he found it difficult to answer one question at a time.

"He lives in the village, in Hartsfoot, sir. At least, his home is here, but I think he works in Brighton most of the time."

"Doing what?"

"I – I don't know," Mallow replied. He realized that this was inadequate. "He has a wife and a son here," he continued. "Since he was demobbed, he seems to have found himself some kind of work in Brighton. It must pay quite well, whatever it is, because he turned up a week or two ago with a decent -looking car."

"Why would he be dealing with the gamekeeper?"

"I don't know, sir. He and Reuben White don't have much in common that I can think of."

"So, what can you tell me about Reuben White?"

"Well, he's the gamekeeper, as I said. He works for the Estate."

"What estate?"

"It used to be owned by Lord Cornfeld before the war, I think he went bust. Anyway, he sold the whole thing, lock, stock and barrel, to some sort of syndicate. It's called something like Consolidated Investments. I don't know much about that."

"You don't seem to know much about anything." The Bear was not inclined to suffer fools gladly. "What about White? Where does he live? Does he have a wife? What does he do as a gamekeeper?"

"He lives in a cottage, the keeper's cottage. It's the other side of The Chase. He lives on his own. His wife died before the war. He has a son, Arthur, but, when Arthur came back from the army, he didn't go back to live with his dad, and he has a flat, I think, in Hazlehurst."

The Bear grunted. "In that case," he said, "you had better come with me in the car so we can break the news to Mrs Champion, and then, if we can find him, to this man's son." He pointed at Reuben White.

He left further instructions with his team. To wait for the doctor himself seemed a bit pointless. The cause of death in each case was obvious enough. Once the bodies could be moved, the two guns could be examined and dusted for prints. The Bear saw no reason to wait: he trusted his team.

IV

Since the constable knew Mrs Champion, though The Bear wondered how well, he left it to him to break the news of her husband's death. She was shaken, but he found it difficult to judge her mood. She was not tearful, and her immediate reaction was to wonder how she would cope financially.

"We shall have to ask you to make a formal identification," he said. "And, since this is an unexpected, not to say suspicious death, there will have to be a post-mortem. It

99

will be some time before the body will be released and you can arrange a funeral."

"Oh dear," she said, "of course, I shall have to arrange a funeral, won't I?"

"Have you got anybody who could help you? Would you want someone to come and keep you company? It's the normal thing. It is a big shock."

Mrs Champion shook her head. "There's no one," she said, "but Percy, my son."

"Percy is ten." The constable explained.

"It will be difficult, telling him," The Bear commented.

"Percy will be relieved, just as I am really."

"Relieved? If you don't mind my saying so, that is a strange reaction."

"Joe isn't, - wasn't a good father or a good husband, Inspector. He treated both of us badly. We were both scared of him, tell the truth."

"That sounds bad."

"Joe was – let's say he was free with his fists, especially when he'd had a drink. Whenever he came home lately, we both dreaded it. It was only when he was busy in his shed or at the pub that we could breathe a bit. He usually got home from the pub at closing time spoiling for a fight."

"Do you know," The Bear asked without guile, "if your husband had a quarrel with Reuben White?"

"The gamekeeper?" Mrs Champion looked very surprised. "I don't think Joe had much to do with him. Nobody in the village had much to do with him. He kept himself to himself."

"What about other people in the village? Did your husband have any enemies? Anybody he had upset?"

Mrs Champion frowned at this. She seemed reluctant to answer.

"Mrs Champion?"

"Well," she said slowly, "it's common knowledge, and someone will tell you sooner or later: he got into a fight with Duncan Frome, the man who bought the Old Forge."

The constable explained a little. "Mr Frome comes from up north. He's only been here for a year. Story goes Joe picked a fight with him and came off worst."

"What was the fight about?"

The constable exchanged glances with Mrs Champion. She answered. "Mr Frome has been very kind to my son," she said. "Percy had got behind at school and Mr Frome has been helping him with his schoolwork. I went to thank him, and Joe got it in his head that there was something going on between us. He gave Percy a good hiding and told him not to go there again. He gave me a black eye, not for the first time either. Then he picked a fight with Mr Frome."

"That was shortly before the fire at the Forge," the constable continued the story. "There was a big, new, wooden shed that Mr Frome had built. It burnt down one night. There was no evidence to show how the fire started, but there were rumours. There are always rumours in a village."

"And these rumours suggested that Mr Champion might be an arsonist?"

"Yes, sir, but, as I say, there was no evidence."

The Bear said nothing. He was thinking. He nodded slowly before he repeated that Mrs Champion would have to make a formal identification of the body, and they would get in touch with her very soon. He led the way out.

"Where do you think we might find Mr White's son?"

"He could be anywhere."

"Does he have a job?"

"Not a regular job, no. He does a bit of gardening, a bit of maintenance, that sort of thing. I don't think he'd be able to hold down a regular job."

"Oh? Why not?"

"Before the war he worked for the Estate, but it was only as a favour to his father by all accounts. He was very unpopular. Even as a boy he had a reputation for bad behaviour. Nobody here would take him on when he got back from the war."

"In that case," said The Bear, "I'm going to leave it to you to track him down. When you have found him, phone this number, and don't let him out of your sight until I get to you. If you have to, keep him at your police house." He wrote down the

Woodbury number on a piece of paper. "No point in wasting my time looking for this man. I'll have a word with Mr Frome."

V

"Mr Frome?" Duncan turned from his workbench and saw a large man standing in the doorway of the Forge.

"Yes? Who wants to know?"

The Bear took out his warrant card and flourished it. "I'm Inspector Blundell," he said. "I'm investigating an incident that took place last night in The Chase" (he assumed that the shooting had taken place the previous evening, and not earlier. The doctor would confirm it no doubt.)

"The Chase? That's the wood, isn't it?"

"I'm sure you know that already, Mr Frome, even though I understand you have not been here all that long."

Duncan nodded, "Just over a year," he said. "But what's this got to do with me?"

"That's what I want to find out," said The Bear. "I believe you had a run-in with a man called Joe Champion."

"What's this about, Inspector?"

"Is it true? You had a fight with the man?"

Duncan nodded again. "Yes, Joe Champion picked a fight with me. He was probably full of beer at the time. It wasn't really much of a fight."

"What was it about?"

103

Duncan's eyes narrowed, wondering what this line of questions was leading to. "The man had a stupid idea that I was getting too friendly with his wife."

"And why did he think that?"

"Mrs Champion came to see me one afternoon to thank me because I've been helping her son, Percy. I've only spoken to the woman once."

"In what way have you been helping the boy?"

"These are very strange questions," Duncan commented. "Percy has shown an interest in the work I do as a mechanic. In return for letting him watch me at work, I insisted that he accepted help with his schoolwork. He had been getting behind."

"Very admirable," said The Bear. The way in which he said it suggested he did not believe it. "I also believe, as part of your eventful few months in Hartsfoot, that you had a serious fire here."

"Yes. A large shed which I used for storage at the back of this plot was burnt down one night."

"An accident?"

"That's what the insurance company thought."

"But you didn't?"

"I take safety very much to heart, Inspector. There was absolutely nothing in that shed likely to start a fire. There was plenty of stuff there to make it burn quickly once it began, but something or someone had to set it off. It wasn't me."

"And you thought it was probably Joe Champion. Is that right?"

"I have no evidence to support that."

"But that's what you thought, wasn't it?"

Duncan did not reply. He looked at the Inspector warily. "Are you going to tell me what this is all about?" he repeated.

"Joe Champion has been found dead."

"Dead?"

"Shot dead."

"Now, hang on a minute!" Duncan was beginning to show signs of anger. The Bear's strategy was beginning to work. "I may have disliked the man – according to Percy he treated him and his wife like a bully, knocking them both about – but there's a difference between finding him offensive and wanting to kill him."

"Just to fill in the gaps," said The Bear, "can you tell me what you were doing yesterday evening, after you finished work here?"

Duncan stared at him, open-mouthed. "Are you asking me if I killed the man?"

"Answer my question," said The Bear. "What were you doing last night? Where were you? And can anybody vouch for you?"

Duncan hesitated. "I went back to my lodgings," he said. "That would be about six o'clock. I got cleaned up and had a meal." He paused, unwilling to go on.

"And then?"

Duncan folded his arms across his chest defiantly. "After that," he said, "I went out, shooting rabbits."

The Inspector nodded gravely. "Did you get any?"

"Three."

"And I take it you have a licence for the gun?"

"Yes."

"And where do you keep it?"

"At my lodgings. The gun used to belong to my landlady's husband."

"No doubt your landlady...?"

"Mrs Cole," Duncan said through his teeth. He made no attempt to conceal his resentment at the questioning and the direction it was leading.

"No doubt Mrs Cole will be able to corroborate the times you went out and came back in?"

"Yes. And I expect she will even show you the rabbits, if you ask her."

"Thank you," said The Bear. "I shall be in touch again, and I will want a statement from you in due course."

From the door of the Old Forge Duncan watched him walk away. He had not been given even the slightest information about the shooting. He wondered what Joe Champion would be doing in the woods. His own situation could be quite suspicious. But surely, if he had been shot while trespassing in The Chase, the more obvious suspect would be the gamekeeper. Hadn't Ruth said that he had a reputation for shooting poachers and asking questions afterwards?

VI

The Bear was very satisfied with his first interview. He was also pleased not to have wasted time. The driver, who had dropped off the village policeman in Hazlehurst, returned to collect him and took him back to The Chase. The doctor had come and gone. A photographer had taken photographs of the crime scene. An ambulance was at the gate when The Bear arrived, and he passed two men with the stretcher carrying one of the bodies. They would have to make a second journey for the other one. As he had hoped, his Sergeant had got them to take the gamekeeper first, giving access to the gun which had been underneath his body. By the time The Bear reached the scene, the gun had been dusted for fingerprints. As might have been expected, they matched the fingerprints taken from the dead man. When, however, the gloved policeman opened the gun, it was still loaded with two cartridges. He removed them carefully and put them in a bag before sniffing the barrel.

"Doesn't seem to have been fired, sir," he said. The Bear sniffed for himself. There was no doubt. The shot which had killed Joe Champion had not come from this gun.

The Sergeant examined the second gun, which had been lying nearly two feet from the outstretched, left hand of Joe Champion. It had been wiped clean of fingerprints. This was becoming extremely complicated. This gun had certainly been fired: both barrels had been used, and there were two used cartridges still in place.

The Bear left his team to work in the woods and drove back to Woodbury. Both bodies would be taken to the morgue here, since there were no facilities in Hazlehurst to carry out a proper post-mortem. The Inspector had to give a preliminary report to the Superintendent. He wanted to get in quickly, but he also wanted time to puzzle out the sequence of events. He was beginning to think that there was only one solution: Joe Champion must have shot the gamekeeper and then turned the gun on himself. If that were so, how had he wiped it clean of prints? He was not wearing gloves. Why would a suicide bother to do that? The position of the used gun was also problematic. If the man had shot himself in the chest, how had he managed to throw the gun clear afterwards? This was not going to be easy.

He reported to the Superintendent. "I have a suspect who might be in the frame," he said. "I'm not sure how or why as yet, but we'll get there."

His chief looked at him with a less than confident air. This sounded like a very complicated case. He would give him a couple of days, after which he might have to look for outside help, he thought.

VII

The post-mortem of Joe Champion's body was carried out the following day, the Superintendent having stated that they needed to establish whether this was, indeed, a suicide. The result was startling. Joe Champion had been blasted by a shot gun at very short range: the spread of shot indicated that it could not have been further than three feet from his chest. This might have supported the idea of a self-inflicted wound, were it not for the fact that a bullet, not shot from a shot gun cartridge, had passed through the heart and had lodged in the spine. This single bullet had almost certainly caused his death, and it was probable that the shot gun wound had occurred post-mortem.

The bullet appeared to have come from a pistol. Immediately he was given this information, The Bear ordered his team to redouble their efforts in the search for the missing weapon. The preliminary search of the immediate area, the clearing itself, had been very thorough. There had been no sign of a third weapon. They needed to extend the search. It took time, there was undergrowth, here and there, there was even the odd patch of brambles. Most of the area was covered in leaf litter. Near the disused rearing pens they found a patch of ground that had been disturbed. Fearing the worst, The Bear ordered his men to excavate it. Only two feet down a spade revealed a bone. Now everyone was tense. The bone, however, was not human: it was the leg bone of an animal. It ended with a hoof, which someone identified as belonging to a deer. More followed. Someone had buried the feet, and more distressingly, the heads of six animals. They were in varying states of decay.

A keen-eyed, young member of the team, a detective constable called Royston, thought he saw evidence of disturbance in the litter on the ground in a space bounded by four trees. To the casual eye there was nothing unusual, but to Royston there was something about the way in which several small twigs seemed to have formed themselves in parallel lines. Someone, he deduced, must have pushed them to one side. Perhaps he had been gathering firewood – unlikely. He looked much more closely, knelt and moved the leaves and twigs gently with his hands. For a moment he was scared, thinking he was close to losing a hand in a hidden trap. He had heard of man traps before. He was sure he had felt hard, metallic edges. Being more cautious, he took a stick and cleared away the leaves. What he found made him stand up and shout, "Sarge!" loudly.

The Sergeant and The Bear arrived in a matter of moments. Royston knew better than to go any further without them. It was the Sergeant who knelt now and carefully brushed away the rest of the leaves. Then, all three men stared in astonishment at what looked like a manhole cover. A manhole cover in the middle of a wood? There were no sewers or other such services within two miles. They stared at their discovery.

"Open it," ordered The Bear.

It was a circular cover, set in a slightly larger, iron square. Unlike any manhole cover he had ever seen before, The Bear realized that this had a handle inset. It was quite heavy, cast-iron, and the Sergeant had to use some force, trying to lift it clear, until he realized it was hinged. It lifted vertically and then fell back to reveal a circular opening. Royston now saw why the twigs had fallen into parallel lines.

"Anyone got a torch?" It seemed an impossible question, but Royston had a torch. He handed it obediently to The Bear. The Inspector lay flat on his belly and shone the light down through the opening.

"How deep is it, sir?" the Sergeant asked.

"I'd say it was about fifteen or sixteen feet deep. But, what's interesting, is what I think I can see at the bottom. Detective," he said to Royston, "you're a bit thinner than I am, take your torch and go down to the bottom. If what I can see is a pistol, we may have found the murder weapon, so for God's sake treat it very carefully, and don't mess up any prints. Have you got a handkerchief on you?"

He had, and it was a clean one. Taking the torch, Royston climbed down the iron rungs of a ladder which was built into the side of the shaft. He got to the bottom and shouted back up, his voice echoing strangely, "It is a pistol, sir, but it looks sort of peculiar" and he proceeded to pick it up in the handkerchief.

"What do you mean, peculiar?" The Bear shouted back.

"It seems to have a funny sort of attachment round the muzzle."

Before he started back up the ladder, he flashed the light around the chamber. He whistled with astonishment, then came quickly to the top.

"I really think you should go and have a look for yourself, sir," he said. "I don't know what this place is, but I've never seen anything like it. It must have something to do with the military."

Before The Bear followed the suggestion, he took a look at the 'peculiar' pistol. The attachment was, he thought, a silencer. This shooting was becoming even more strange. Why would anybody want to use a silencer in a wood, which a gamekeeper patrolled with a gun? Anybody within earshot, hearing a gun, would assume it was a perfectly legitimate event. The gamekeeper would be shooting wild birds or vermin of one sort or another.

The Inspector and the Sergeant, with the aid of Royston's torch, now descended into the depths. Like the Detective Constable, they, too, were astonished. They were in a bunker, an underground room. It was just over 10 feet long and 8 feet wide, and high enough to stand up in. There was a crude table and shelves on the wall. There was a quantity of tinned food, meat, vegetables and fruit, tins of condensed milk, sugar, tea, and a dozen large bottles of water. A primus stove stood on the table. The provisions would keep a man adequately fed for some time.

What had caused Royston to use the word military was the equipment stored on the shelves and on the floor. There was a Tommy gun, and metal ammunition boxes. When The Bear opened one, he found it neatly packed with explosives at one end and, at the other, fuses. A second box contained serious - looking ammunition, not ordinary bullets or cartridges, but what looked like anti-tank rockets. It was the last box which gave an even greater surprise: it was full of money, white fivers and pound notes.

"What do you think this is all about, sir?" the Sergeant asked.

"I haven't a clue, Sergeant. I think Detective Royston may have unearthed something hush-hush. Just to be on the safe side, keep this strictly to yourself. I'll put the fear of God into Royston. This has all the hallmarks of MI5 or something. What the hell it's doing here in the middle of a wood, God alone knows."

The two men climbed to the surface. They replaced the manhole cover and covered it with leaves. They had retrieved only the pistol.

VIII

The discovery of the bunker was to lead to unforeseen complications. The Bear, having ordered both the Sergeant and Royston not to mention it to anybody else, nevertheless informed his superior. The information was passed rapidly upwards and, within an hour, and order came back from an office in Whitehall: no one must be told of this on pain of prosecution, and the three policemen who had discovered the bunker were to make themselves available for briefing as soon as a car could bring a Mr Jones to speak to them.

Mr Jones was a grey man in a grey suit. He had the well-groomed look of a city dweller. He flashed an identity card of some sort to the desk sergeant, and he was taken straight to the Superintendent's office. Within minutes the three men were called in.

"I trust you have kept this discovery to yourselves?"

All three of them nodded.

"Good. I imagine you are very curious to know what this is all about. However, before I can tell you, I am going to ask each of you, including your Superintendent here, to sign a document. It refers to the Official Secrets Act. Once you have signed this document, you will be aware that to reveal any of the information I give you could result in very long prison sentences, in some cases life, and in the very worst cases, a death sentence for treason."

All four men were taken completely by surprise. They all looked shocked, but, having no choice, each man looked at the piece of paper presented to him, scanned it quickly, and signed, not without trepidation.

"Good," said Mr Jones. "None of what I am about to tell you can become public knowledge. You cannot tell your colleagues or even your wives. I cannot emphasise that enough."

"I have a question," said The Bear. "We are investigating a double murder, and it looks as though the pistol we found in the bunker was a murder weapon. When we bring the murderer to justice, how are we to explain where we found the weapon?"

"That's your problem. You can concoct any story you like, but you may not reveal the truth."

The Bear said nothing. He did not like the prospect of being unable to state "the truth, the whole truth", and was already concerned that this limitation might make a prosecution more difficult.

"You will remember," said Mr Jones, "just how close the Germans came to invading Britain. After Dunkirk the War Cabinet had very serious doubts about our ability to withstand a full-blooded invasion across the Channel. The enemy was only 22 miles away. Mr Churchill devised a scheme, involving what were called 'Auxiliary Units', civilians, many of them in the country. Their task, after an invasion, was to sabotage the occupying force in any way they could. These Auxiliaries were given training in unarmed combat, in the use of explosives, in the use of small arms, and even equipped with anti-tank rockets. What you have stumbled across is one such unit. I imagine that your gamekeeper friend was trained."

"That's incredible!" the Superintendent said.

"A small detachment will come down tomorrow and retrieve all the weaponry from the bunker. Please make sure that all your men except yourselves, are cleared from the wood between the hours of 1400 and 1800."

"We'll have to hang on to the pistol; it's evidence," The Bear said.

"Very well, but you cannot reveal where you found it."

"It appears to have a silencer fitted," The Bear said.

Mr Jones nodded. "That's standard," he said. "War is a dirty business."

When he had gone, and with the impending visit of an army squad to think about, The Bear took two men to look over the keeper's cottage. He was not sure if a search would tell him anything, but it was just one those things he thought he should do. There had been no keys on the body, but they were not necessary: the door was unlocked. It was a thatched, flint-built building. The doors and windows were painted the familiar green, but the paint was flaking and old. The windows were filthy. The floors were not much better. They were covered in linoleum, on top of which there were one or two rugs, so discovered that it was impossible to tell their original colour. In the kitchen, the top of the range showed signs of spills. There were dirty dishes in the sink and the table was cluttered with cutlery, sauce bottles, a cheap cruet set on an oilcloth covering.

The Bear was not interested in the kitchen. He noticed that water was piped to a tap. Outside the back door he found a wooden handle, which was attached to a pump mechanism. Water must have been pumped up into a tank. There was also a large zinc bath hanging on the wall. He wondered if the gamekeeper ever used it.

He was more interested in the contents of the sitting room and the bedrooms, of which there were two. Only one appeared to be in use. The bedclothes, like the floor coverings, were of indiscriminate colour. The sitting room contained to old armchairs, a simple table with three upright chairs, and nothing else of note. On either side of the open fireplace there were built in cupboards. The doors of these cupboards were wide open, and the contents had been partly discarded onto the floor. Three grimy prints had been removed from the walls, leaving lighter patches on the dark green paper. A bookshelf, containing a variety of old books, also covered in dust, had also been emptied onto the floor.

"Looks as though someone's given this place are going-over," the Sergeant observed.

The Bear agreed. "I wonder what he was looking for. I wonder who it was, for that matter. This place is so off the beaten track, how many people know where it is, I wonder. Maybe the keeper's son can tell us, if the village copper ever catches up with him, that is. We may have to look for him ourselves, I reckon."

Unlike the front door, the door to the lean-to was locked. However, the key was easily found, it was hanging on a rusty nail in the kitchen. They entered. Like many old cottages of this type, this room had been built so that the inhabitants could use it to slaughter a pig once a year. It was common practice to keep a pig, and to cure the meat, salting it down and hanging the hams in the chimney to smoke. A second animal would be ready to replace the first one. There were two deer carcasses hanging from large, old, iron hooks in the beams. It gave the room a spooky feel. The floor sloped to a central gutter, so that blood, and water used to wash down the floor, could drain through a hole in the wall. Under the window there was a wooden workbench. It incorporated a large sink and a pipe led from a tap up across the ceiling and into the wall of the cottage itself. No doubt it was connected to a water tank there. On the bench were all the implements used by a butcher, gleaming knives, a saw, and a heavy-duty cleaver. The bench itself was made of very sturdy timber, probably beech. In a corner there was a bucket and a yard broom, together with a can of Jeyes

Fluid. The gamekeeper clearly tried to keep the place as sterile as possible. Nevertheless, it had an unpleasant odour.

"This place," the Sergeant said, "looks almost like a professional butcher's shop."

"Yes, and our friend, White, was probably quite skilled. He obviously took the job seriously. He must have been making quite a lot of money out of it."

There was nothing much more to see, but The Bear left with the impression that this was more than a casual poacher at work. This was a professional criminal.

This was another complication, one which might well have a bearing on the murder investigation. For the moment, however, they had to get back to The Chase.

A small army truck arrived just after 14:00 hours. There were four men. They did not drive through the village, but the driver chose the long way round via Belham to arrive at the opposite side of the wood. As instructed, The Bear had removed all his men, sending them off on other duties. One of the four soldiers had two pips on his shoulder: they were obviously taking this very seriously.

"Inspector?" he said.

"Yes, that's me."

"Take us to the bunker," he commanded. "Our orders are to remove all the weaponry. Once we have done that, we shall make sure that the entrance to the bunker is properly concealed. No one must enter it again, and, of course, you may not talk about it to anyone."

The Bear was not happy. He and his two fellow-policemen led the way, and then watched as the bunker was systematically emptied. A Tommy gun and a rifle came first, then the ammunition was hoisted up the shaft. The metal cases with their contents were extremely heavy, but the men had come prepared with suitable ropes. The policemen watched as the pile of ammunition cases grew. The last one was the one containing money.

"I'm not sure," said the officer, "what this is doing here. This has nothing to do with the Auxiliary Unit. What has been going on?"

"That is what we are trying to find out," said The Bear.

."I think," said the officer, "we had better count money. You had better take charge of it. I shall need a receipt."

"Very well," said The Bear, "but how the hell are we supposed to explain it? We can't say where we found it."

The officer merely shrugged. "Your problem," he said.

They counted the money. There was £1850 in notes. The day, thought The Bear, was getting more and more confusing. He could hardly donate all this money to the Benevolent Fund. He had signed an official receipt for it, so would be held responsible for it, if any went missing. All he could do was to take it back to the nick, and keep it safely locked away for now.

The four soldiers, including the officer, carried everything back to their truck. They had to make eight trips; the ammunition cases were especially heavy, but, The Bear did not offer to help. He felt a deep sense of resentment. He watched as two of the men ensured that the manhole cover was disguised with leaves and twigs and dirt until it was invisible once more, and then, without a word, the party withdrew. The policemen heard the truck rev up and leave.

IX

The Chase was quite a long way from the village. That meant that it was going to be extremely difficult to find witnesses to this unusual double-shooting. Duncan Frome had motive and opportunity for killing one of the victims, namely Joe Champion. He was also used to using a shot gun. But why would he want to kill the gamekeeper? And why would he use the same shot gun – not his own – to kill both men? But that wasn't the case either: Champion had been shot through the heart with a pistol, probably the pistol retrieved from the bunker. It was enough to torment The Bear.

The Frost farm was the closest habitation to the murder scene. Maybe Dorothy Frost or her son could shed some light on the comings and goings. They might at the very least have seen the gamekeeper from time to time, possibly even on the evening or night in question. They would surely have heard the shots.

Initial enquiries in the village had given various information about the Frosts, although the fact that Jack Frost was illegitimate had been made clear in disapproving tones. When The Bear knocked on the door of the farm, it was opened by Dorothy. He introduced himself and showed his warrant card. Dorothy looked frightened, he thought.

"Mrs Frost," he said, "May I come in?"

"What's this about?" She stood back to allow him into the kitchen, and gestured to a seat at the large table. The Bear was thinking about the squalid kitchen in the gamekeeper's cottage, and was very aware of the contrast here.

"You have probably heard that there has been a serious incident in The Chase."

"No. I've been busy on the farm for the past week, and I haven't been into the village. What kind of incident?"

"Someone has been shot."

"Oh no! It was bound to happen one day."

"What makes you say that?"

"The gamekeeper, Reuben White, is a nasty piece of work. He patrols that wood with a gun, and people say he doesn't hesitate to shoot. There's a message on the gate that has been there as long as I can remember, warning people that trespassers will be shot. He means it."

"Do you hear any shooting in the woods from here?"

"Yes, quite often."

"Can you think back to the night before last? Did you hear any shots then?"

Dorothy Frost thought for a moment. "Yes, it was late on," she said. "I thought it was a bit strange. Why would anybody be shooting at that time? But I didn't really give it much thought."

"Well," said The Beast," it wasn't Reuben White. He won't be doing any more shooting. He was the one shot."

Dorothy looked shocked.

"How many shots did you hear?"

"How many? I'm not sure. I didn't count them. More than one. Maybe there were just two. He probably fired both barrels."

"It's your son about? Maybe he heard something."

Dorothy's reaction to this innocent request was extreme; she looked very alarmed. "Jack? What you want with him? He can't tell you anything that I can't."

"You never know, Mrs Frost. " He's a young man, I understand, and he may have sharper hearing. If he's not too far away perhaps you could ask him to come in – or I can even go and speak to him where he is working." He paused. Dorothy Frost did not move. She looked uncomfortable. The Bear added casually, "Does your son use a gun as well?"

At this, Dorothy looked even more concerned. She was acting almost guiltily. "Very occasionally," she admitted. "He's very careful." Reluctantly she stood up. "I'll go and get him," she said. "It will take me a few minutes. He is working in Six Acres."

The Bear assumed this was the name of a field. He stood up but did not follow her. From the doorway he watched her as she walked with the purposeful stride of a man across the field next to the farmhouse. Jack, who was working on the far side of the field, was bent over, but he straightened up as his mother approached. No doubt she must have called out to him. She spoke to him the Bear was too far away to hear any part of the conversation, but it was animated, the young man was gesticulating angrily. He appeared to be shaking his head. This confrontation continued for perhaps two minutes until Jack threw down the implement he had in his hand. He did so with some violence, before following his mother back to the farmhouse.

The Bear retreated into the kitchen, not wanting to reveal that he had watched. At the door mother and son both removed their boots before coming in. Dorothy introduced her son.

The Bear wasted no time in preliminaries. "What is your relationship with the gamekeeper, Reuben White?" he asked.

"I mean how well do you know him, how often do you talk to him, what about, whether you and he are friendly or hostile."

At this, there was a perceptible change: Jack look almost relieved for some, inexplicable reason. "I don't know Reuben White except by sight," he said. "I've never spoken to him. I don't have much to do with the village. I've only moved in here a little while ago."

"But you do know Reuben White by sight?"

"Yes."

"When was the last time you saw him?"

"I can't remember exactly. I was with mum. We were shopping in Hazlehurst and he parked in front of us."

"And you haven't seen him since?"

"Well, I have seen him a couple of times in The Chase."

The Bear's eyes lit up at this. "You've been into the wood?"

"No, I never go inside The Chase. I believe Mr White is likely to shoot first and ask questions afterwards. I've seen him on the edges of the wood a couple of times. Maybe he was inspecting the fences."

This appeared to be going nowhere. The Bear asked one or two more questions, then left.

X

The Superintendent pulled a long face. "This case is far too complicated for you, Inspector. Unfortunately, I don't have much choice in the matter. Discovering that blasted bunker has put the cat among the pigeons. If we called in help, we wouldn't be free to tell him where we found that pistol. It wouldn't be fair to expect someone to pick up this case without access to all the facts." He sighed, leaned back in his chair, looked hard in the direction of The Bear, and attempted to sum up. "What we have is a double murder. Two men, apparently shot with the same gun, a shot gun, but one of them also shot by a pistol . One victim, the gamekeeper, was killed by the shot gun, the second, a man called Joe Champion, was killed with the pistol, then shot again with the shot gun, apparently in a clumsy attempt to disguise the pistol wound. We don't know whether both men were killed by the same person. It's possible that the gamekeeper was killed by Champion, who was then, himself killed by a third person. Certainly, there has to be a third person involved, and he has to be responsible for the death of Champion at least.

"This third person must have had access to the secret bunker. How could he know about it? It could be that he was one of this so-called Auxiliary Unit. We are not going to get any help from the security people they are not going to tell us the names of members of that unit. We do, at least, have a good set of prints from the pistol, that will only help us when we have found and identified a suspect.

"You have so far identified two men, each of whom has a motive to kill one of the two victims. Duncan Frome had some reason to resent Champion, believing him to be responsible for the fire which destroyed his building. It seems there was personal antagonism between them, something to do with Frome's relationship with Champion's son, and possibly with his wife.

"Mrs Frost and her son, Jack, also had strong reasons to hate the gamekeeper, Reuben White. Either of them could have shot him, but would they kill Champion?"

It was a fair summing-up, and The Bear had nothing to add. The Super scratched his head. "You'll just have to carry on as best you can," he said, not attempting to disguise his regret. The Inspector did not take offence; he was aware that he was in over his head this time. He could only try, and he would be relieved, in a sense, to be reporting frequently because it shifted the responsibility from his shoulders to those of the grizzle-headed Superintendent.

"Keep looking for the gamekeeper's son," he said. "If, as people say, he is an unreliable character, he may have a hand in this, too."

"It's our first priority, sir," The Bear acknowledged.

"Find out what you can about this man, Champion. He sounds a very dodgy character, too. How did he spend his days in Brighton? We'll get some help there, but it would make things a little easier if we knew even the slightest thing about it.

"And what's this about the venison? How did White get rid of it? Was he selling it locally? Are all the villagers secretly eating off the fat of the land, so to speak, while the rest of us make do with rations?"

"Venison's a very lean meat, sir," The Bear observed solemnly.

The Superintendent gave him a straight look, suspecting sarcasm, then sighed as he realized the man was simply a fool. He dismissed him then and reached for a bottle of aspirin tablets.

XI

Mervyn Hardcastle was surprised, but he opened the door and said, "You'd better come in, Inspector."

The Bear followed him into the sitting room, and both men sat down.

"I understand, sir," he said, "that you were in charge of the local Home Guard."

"Yes, Inspector?"

"Well, sir, we have a difficult, or should I say delicate problem to deal with. You understand that we are investigating the deaths of two men?"

"Yes, of course. Inspector, but what has that to do with me or the Home Guard ?"

The Bear hesitated, looked distinctly uncomfortable, then plunged in. "As the local Captain," he said, "you would be the local contact for the Auxiliary Unit."

Mervyn Hardcastle was taken aback. Joviality gave way to a frown. "Inspector," he said, "I have no idea how you came to hear about Auxiliary Units, but you should not be talking about them openly to anyone, including myself. I suspect that even mentioning the words could render you liable to prosecution under the Official Secrets Act."

"That's why I said the matter was delicate, sir. The fact is, the perpetrator of at least one of the murders must have known about this Unit. He clearly gained access. Unless I know the names of members of this Unit, I shall remain handicapped. Is there any way -?"

But it was clear from the expression on Mervyn Hardcastle's face, that he was flogging a dead horse. The frown remained and the muscles around mouth and chin were tense.

"I cannot help you, Inspector," he said, "and I would strongly advise you not to mention this subject again to anybody. I must ask you to leave."

And that was that. The Bear left, none the wiser. From Hardcastle's reaction, nonetheless, it was clear that he at least knew of the Auxiliary Unit. Surely, he could not be involved? He had the means; what possible motive could he have?

XII

It took a while to discover Arthur White's whereabouts. He had gone to ground. At last, one of the more diligent members of The Bear's team got the name of a man who had served with Arthur White. He tracked him down and learned that White's closest friend had been a Private Burke. Burke hailed from Guildford. A telephone call to the Guildford police alerted them to the search for Arthur White and the missing van. Within a few hours a constable, walking his normal beat, reported that he had found a van with the Estate logo. It was parked in a side street. CID took over and two men, one at the front door and one at the back, began their enquiries where the van was parked. Burke opened the door. White was inside. He was arrested on the charge of taking a vehicle without the owner's permission, and driving it without insurance. The Bear sent a car to collect him.

"Mr White," The Bear began, "when did you last see your Father?"

"About ten days ago."

"I have to give you some bad news."

"What news is that?"

"Your father has met with an accident."

"What kind of accident?"

"I'm afraid he has been shot." The Bear watched closely, hoping, even expecting to learn something from the reaction to this news. It might indeed not be news at all, if Arthur White had been present at the fatal shooting. He appeared to be shocked at the news, but not to profoundly shocked. Was it real, The Bear wondered? He could not be sure. He waited for Arthur White to respond.

"How did it happen?" he said at last. "An accident? He was very careful. He used that gun every day."

"What gun is that?"

"His favourite gun. It's a shotgun, twelve-bore, double-barrelled."

"We don't think it was an accident."

"What d'you mean?"

"We believe he was deliberately shot and killed."

Arthur did not look especially surprised by this news. He said nothing for a moment, then, "Who did it?" he sked.

" That is what we are trying to find out." The Bear had learned very little from this exchange. He continued with the interview on a different tack. "In the course of our enquiries into your father's death," he said," we went to his cottage. It had clearly been ransacked, and we then noticed that his van was missing. You had taken the van. Why? And can we assume that it was you who searched the cottage?"

Arthur White stared back at him defiantly. "Okay, yes, it was me."

"You searched the cottage?"

"Yes."

"What exactly were you looking for?"

Arthur thought for a moment, frowning down at the table. Then, he said slowly, "I take it you looked in the shed?"

"What do you mean by the shed?"

"The lean-to bit, the part of the cottage with a separate door."

"Yes, we did look in there."

"It's all set up like a proper butcher's shop," Arthur said. "My dad has a profitable side-line, selling deer meat. It's breaking the law, of course. The deer belong to the Estate really.

He keeps all the money. When I found out about it, I told him he should give me some of the money to keep my mouth shut."

"But he didn't?"

"No. He's a mean bastard. You'd think he would look after his own, wouldn't you?"

"Are you telling me you stole money from your own father after breaking into his house?"

"I didn't break in. I knew he always left the door open. And no, I didn't steal any money because I didn't find any."

"So why did you take the van and drive off?"

"You never knew my father, I take it? If you did, you wouldn't be asking the question. When I was a kid, he would take his belt to me, the buckle end! I wouldn't like to guess what he would have done if he had found me trying to steal from him. I needed to get away as far as I could."

This put a new light on things.

"Seeing as how you were so scared of your father," The Bear continued, "weren't you taking a risk, going to his cottage?"

"I waited till he left for work."

"How did you know he'd left home?"

"I watched."

"But weren't you afraid of being seen?"

"No. You forget I grew up in The Chase. I learned a thing or two from my dad, like how to move about without being seen. You need to do that when you're stalking deer – or anything else."

"You didn't follow him ?"

"Why would I do that? He knows - knew the woods better than anyone, including me, and why would I, anyway? I told you, my first thought was to get away. He always left the keys in the van."

"He seems to have been very careless about security."

"Suppose so. I was mad about not finding his money."

"So, where do you think he could have hidden it?"

Arthur shrugged. "If I knew that," he said, "I'd be in Bermuda by now."

He was too sure of himself for The Bear's liking. "You say you spent a lot of your time in The Chase," he said. "How well would you say you know it?"

"Pretty well as well as my dad."

"Like the back of your hand?"

"You could say that."

"Right. I shall now charge you with taking away a motor vehicle without the owner's consent, and with driving while uninsured. I have no reason to keep you here, but you must remain where we can contact you. I assume you will want to begin the arrangements for your father's funeral, but it will be a while before that can happen."

"Oh! Why?"

"There has to be time to complete our enquiries, and they may involve further work for the coroner."

The Bear suspected the delay was not altogether unwelcome to Arthur White, who would probably find it hard to get enough money together to bury his father. Even the cottage was not his, and he had no idea where the profits of the illegal trade were. The paperwork was completed: White would appear before the magistrates in three days' time.

PART THREE

Earthquakes and aftershocks.

I

Brenda Dampier was growing daily more impatient with her husband. He seemed to have lost almost all his enthusiasm for pastoral work. At times she suspected that his faith was less strong than it used to be. The war had taken its toll. He looked much older and had begun to behave more like an old man. At times he was strangely irrational. She noted that the day he devoted to preparing his weekly sermon now depressed rather than inspired him. As for the sermons themselves, they had changed from amusing and interesting to dry, academic, Biblical studies. He was going through the motions. As far as their marital life was concerned, it was becoming little better than two old friends – no, two old acquaintances – sharing the same house. They had little to say to one another.

She had always been ready to share the pastoral care. She enjoyed it. It brought her into contact with the villagers, especially the women, and she thought of them as friends. Thus, the news of Joe Champion's sudden death turned her thoughts to his widow, Peggy. She must be into her forties now. She had married Joe at the age of thirty in 1938. Everyone thought she had been left on the shelf by then, and that was the most likely reason she had married Joe. He was not a good catch, but he had a house, which he rented, so could provide a home. He also fathered their child, Percy, a child Brenda found it difficult to like. He was, to put it frankly, out of control. Peggy had no idea how to discipline a child, indulging him instead. He was a little terror, and not a likeable terror, either.

It had not occurred to Graham Dampier, not yet anyway, to call on Peggy Champion. He would wake up to that part of his duty, no doubt, when required to officiate at the funeral. Brenda took it upon herself to call, but she was unsure of the reception she might receive. She spoke to Grace Cole and asked her to go with her. Grace had known Peggy since she was a small girl, far longer than she, Brenda, had.

Brenda pushed her bike as Grace walked with her the short distance to the Champions' cottage. Attached to the handlebars was a basket containing a paper bag full of cheese scones which she had made specially. She knocked on the door. It was opened by Percy, who took a surprised look at the two visitors, turned his back on them without speaking, and shouted, "Mum! It's that Mrs Dampier and old Mrs Cole!"

Peggy came hurriedly to the door without reprimanding the boy for his rudeness. She looked flustered. She was wiping floured hands on her apron.

"Oh!" she said. "Are you collecting for something?"

Brenda explained the purpose of the visit, to make sure the two of them were all right. She had brought some cheese scones. Perhaps they might come in? A cup of tea, perhaps? Peggy, accustomed to obedience by her husband, stammered her acceptance, and the three women entered the front room. It was sparsely furnished, and they sat at the table, with its thick, chenille cloth. Percy followed them in.

It was a difficult conversation at first. The two visitors were at pains to express their sympathy, not entirely sure that it was appropriate in this case. Although Peggy had been widowed, her husband had not been a source of understanding

138

or comfort. What's more, she did not appear to be particularly distressed by his death.

"To tell you the truth," she admitted, "it's more of a relief than anything. I can hardly believe he's gone, of course. It hasn't really sunk in yet. I half expect to see him come crashing through the door, ready to give me or Percy here a slap, if we say anything out of turn."

Although this is what both women had suspected, this frank statement was shocking.

"If you don't mind my saying so," Grace Cole observed," you sound almost afraid of him, of your own husband!"

Peggy and Percy both nodded vigorously at this. "We were!" Peggy said. "We never knew quite what to expect, did we, Percy?"

"I knew what to expect," Percy contradicted her. "I'm glad he's not coming back."

"You really shouldn't be saying things like that about your own father," Brenda Dampier said reproving him.

"Why not? It's the truth. Shouldn't I tell the truth?"

Brenda was nonplussed. There was no real answer to this. She frowned into her teacup.

"I think one or two of us," Grace Cole said, hoping to smooth over the awkwardness," had our suspicions that all was not well."

The awkwardness remained in the small silence that followed.

"Some of the time," Peggy said," Joe would disappear into his shed and spend hours down there. We were always on edge then, waiting for him to come back. It was a prohibited area for us. He always kept the shed locked, and I have no idea what he did there, probably drank a lot of beer. So far I haven't screwed up the courage even to look inside it."

"Can I go and look?" Percy suggested eagerly.

"No, not until I've had a look first. I don't know what's in there."

This was a strange conversation; Grace and Brenda exchanged glances, not knowing what to say.

"Now I've got witnesses," Peggy said, "I think we should go and look."

The two women were disconcerted by all this, but they could do little except follow Peggy and her son out of the back door and down the garden path. Halfway down was the infamous shed. From the outside it appeared innocent enough. It was a simple, garden shed, about eight feet square, with a door in the side and a window. On the door itself there was a very large padlock through a metal hasp.

"I don't know where the key is," said Peggy, "but if we hit this thing with a brick or something, it will probably come out of the door."

She looked around for something hard and heavy, but Percy had already found a rusting spade stuck in the soil. He didn't hand it over, instead he swung it at the padlock. The force of the blow pulled the four securing screws of the hasp away from the door, whereupon Peggy grabbed the padlock and gave it a strong, final pull. It came away easily, and the door swung open about six inches. Even Percy was not quick enough to beat her to the door. She pulled it open far enough to look inside, blocking the view for everyone else.

Peggy stepped inside. The others followed her. A piece of sacking had been draped over the window. It was obviously intended to prevent people from looking in, since the view was only of a vegetable patch. Peggy tore it down. There was no electric light, but now the inside of the hut was exposed, and it was not very attractive. There was a bench under the window, a kitchen chair, and an extremely old armchair. There was no other furniture. On the wall above the workbench, to one side of the window, there was pinned a lurid calendar with a glossy picture of a naked woman. Peggy tore that down too. The edge of the bench had numerous burn marks where the occupant had left cigarettes smouldering. There was also an overflowing ashtray and a metal box about eighteen inches long, slightly less wide and a foot deep. It was padlocked. There were numerous, old newspapers and magazines, many of them on the floor. It had not been swept for long time.

"What's in the box?" Percy asked.

Peggy stepped outside the shed for a moment and came back with the spade. With one swift blow she broke the padlock. The others watched as she opened the box. She gasped. The two women leaned forward to see what she had discovered, but it was just a little too high for Percy to see.

"Where did all this come from?" Peggy asked in disbelief. She was looking at a large pile of banknotes. There were a lot of big, white five-pound notes, and so many pound notes they could not guess at their value.

"We'll have to take these indoors and count them," Brenda said. "Then, we shall have to tell the police."

"You think it's all stolen money?" Peggy was unable to think straight.

"Unless your husband had a huge win on the Pools, what other explanation is there?"

Percy was dancing up and down with impatience. "What is it?" he asked.

"More money than I have ever seen in my life," his mother said. "I wish it was ours!"

"Well, can't we keep some of it? It is in our shed."

"No!" The three women spoke as one. Percy shrugged. He could not understand.

Back in the house, Peggy put a tea towel on the table to protect it, then put the metal box on top. Percy joined the three women at the table, and watched, wide-eyed with excitement, as his mother took handfuls of paper money from the box and put it on the table to begin counting. Half hidden by some of the notes, there was a biscuit tin also in the box. She left that for the time being and, assisted by the two women, she began counting. She picked out all the five-pound notes first and stacked them neatly. They agreed that they amounted to £1,700. The pound notes took a lot longer to count. She stacked them in piles of

£100. There were forty-one piles altogether, as well as a small stack of thirty – a total of £4,130. Added to the five pound notes, this made a total value of £5,830, a small fortune, enough to buy several houses. Brenda carefully wrote down the totals on a piece of cheap stationery, provided by Peggy. All three women were stupefied.

Peggy told Percy to go and find a shopping bag from the kitchen. She put all the money into it. For a few minutes they just sat and stared at the bag; they were all at a loss as to what to do next.

"I don't want this here," Peggy said. "I don't like it. What if we were robbed?"

"The sooner you get it to the police, the better," Grace Cole suggested.

"How do we get it there? I haven't got a car, and I don't fancy taking all this on a bus all the way to Woodbury."

"Oh, but you do have a car, Joe's car: the police have finished with it, and it's with Mr Frome at the workshop."

"Have we really got a car?" Percy asked.

"I had forgotten about that," Peggy said. "But I don't drive anyway."

"Mr Frome would probably drive it," Percy suggested. The three women looked at him.

"He probably would, you know," Grace Cole agreed.

"Before you do anything else," Brenda said, "perhaps you should finish the job, and empty the box completely."

Peggy was almost afraid of what she would find in the biscuit tin. She now took it from the box. A piece of paper adhered to the underside of the tin, and she pulled it off. It seemed to be an invoice, or something of the kind. At the top was printed a business address, Julian Green, Antiques and Objets d'Art, and an address in Brighton. There was no other writing, but Peggy turned the paper over, almost without thinking. On the back there was what looked like a diagram or plan, with a few scribbled words here and there. She put it back into the box and turned her attention to the biscuit tin.

The tin had rattled when she moved it, so she assumed it would contain coins. Instead, it contained a quantity of jewellery. It sparkled. With a kind of awe Peggy picked up a diamond tiara and placed it reverently on the table. It was followed by a matching, diamond necklace, two pendants on exquisite gold chains, four bracelets, also of gold, six brooches containing opals, emeralds, more diamonds, and a topaz. Finally, there were five pairs of earrings, three containing pearls.

They were reduced to silence, and for a long time stared at all this beauty. Peggy was thoroughly confused: she loved the jewellery, but she was horror-struck that her husband had been a jewel thief. The other two women were contemplating the scale of this theft.

None of them could attempt to value this treasure, but they all suspected it was worth more than the cash. It was a responsibility which none of them wanted, and they all agreed Peggy must get rid of it as quickly as possible.

Duncan Frome, when Grace contacted him by telephone, after returning home, leaving the other two women with Percy to guard the treasure, said yes, he would happily drive them to Woodbury Police Station. In fact, he said, striking a curiously light note, he had been itching to try out Joe Champion's car. If he liked it, he said, he might even buy it from Peggy.

Within the hour Percy and his mother were sitting in the back seat of the black car, being driven to the police station. Peggy handed over the box and its contents. It took longer than she expected, because the contents had to be itemised and she was given a receipt. She was then asked to make a statement, detailing how she had discovered the box. The Bear had been informed of this development and was interested to hear the story for himself. He thanked her. She was a little puzzled when he showed great interest in the invoice which had been stuck to the bottom of the biscuit tin.

It was late in the evening by the time they got back to Hartsfoot. It had been exhausting for Peggy, but Percy was still seething with excitement. He continued to question the need to hand over the treasure to the police. As he drove homewards, Duncan tried his best to explain. Percy listened and appeared to accept what he was told; he had great respect for Mr Frome. He had been a very good friend, and he knew an awful lot about engines and things. All the same, it seemed a shame to hand over all that money.

II

Peggy got up at daybreak. Thoughts thrashed around in her head. The angry gap between Joe and his wife had meant little meaningful conversation. Peggy felt no loyalty towards him, no regret at his death. Had he been a successful or popular figure, she would have felt no pride. She was angry, uncertain and anxious.

Her anxiety was aggravated when, as she was giving her son breakfast, another police car arrived. Two plain-clothes officers presented their warrant cards, together with a piece of paper which authorised them to search the premises.

"What for?" she asked indignantly.

"I don't know exactly, madam," the taller of the two said, "Maybe it's just in case you've missed something."

"Do you think I've kept something for myself?"

The search was thorough and embarrassing. Peggy watched as the two men systematically searched cupboards and drawers, including her personal clothing. They lifted the mattress on her bed and on Percy's. They climbed steps and looked in the small loft. They even rolled back the lino which covered the living room floor and checked for loose floorboards. Then they left.

III

"Oh dear!" .said Grace Cole as she put down the phone. "Ruth has been fired. She's been complaining that the other drivers, the men, are paid more than she is, because she's a woman."

"So, what's she going to do now?" Duncan asked. He had only just returned from driving the Champions.

"Well, she says she's coming home tomorrow. It will be nice to have her, of course, but I don't know what she is going to do for work. There's not much call for drivers in Hartsfoot."

"How's she getting home?"

"She's coming by train and catching the bus from Hazlehurst."

"Did she say what time?"

"She reckons she'll be in Hazlehurst by half past two. Why do you ask?"

"I'll meet the train and pick her up."

"Oh, that would be good. Thank you. I'll ring her back and let her know."

There was too much happening, thought Grace. All this business with Peggy Champion and all that money and stolen stuff. That was bad enough on top of two men dead. There must be a connection surely. Now Ruth was coming home with her problems. It was all just a little too much. She was suddenly grateful that Duncan Frome was around to lend a hand at such times.

Duncan had agreed to buy the car from Peggy. The money would come in handy for her. She wasn't sure how she was going to cope without the modest housekeeping which Joe had provided, when he remembered. She imagined she would get some kind of widow's pension, but that would probably not be enough to live on. The money from the car would not last for ever, but Mr Frome had given her a decent price for it, enough, if needs be, to keep them going for at least a year. She would probably have to find herself a job, something she had not thought about before. It would probably have to be in Hazlehurst.

Duncan was waiting for the train the following afternoon. He was not at all sure what mood Ruth would be in. He half expected her to be downcast at having lost her job. He did not expect her to be full of the joys of spring, but she was. She greeted him gaily as he took her two suitcases and put them in the boot.

"Good to see you," he said, "even if the circumstances aren't that great."

"The job, you mean? Well, it was a matter of principle. I was doing at least as good a job as anybody else, so why did they pay me less? It's not fair, and I said so. You've got to stand up for yourself these days."

"Very true," Duncan agreed, staring carefully out into the main road and heading homewards. "So, have you any special plans?"

"Not really. I might as well enjoy being at home for a week or two. I'll keep my eyes open for any jobs."

"I've had an idea." Duncan sounded tentative.

"Oh yes?"

"I know you said you didn't really want to come back to Hartsfoot, but I can offer you a job."

"You?"

"Yes, the business is beginning to work quite well, and I want to expand. Once the extension to the workshop is completed, and I have an inspection pit, I want to take on more repair and maintenance work. There's too much work for one man and I'll need someone to help me."

"I know I said I was interested in being a mechanic, but I don't know enough for that."

"No, I understand, but I can offer you a proper apprenticeship."

This was something unexpected. Ruth was silent for a while as they drove steadily towards Hartsfoot. "I need to think it over," she said.

"Of course. It's a serious offer, but it would mean your staying in Hartsfoot. But you would be properly qualified at the end of it. Think about it."

He changed the subject. Ruth had already heard a very brief account of the goings-on in Peggy Champion's life. Her mother had started to tell her about the discovery of the money and jewellery, but Ruth had been preoccupied with telling her mother about her job. Now Duncan told her a little more, taking care not to over-dramatize the whole thing.

"Gosh! What's happening to our little village?"

There wasn't an answer.

They were very nearly home. Duncan was concentrating on his driving, but Ruth looked along the little lane towards Peggy Champion's house. It was no more than fifty yards from the road, and clearly visible. She looked out of curiosity.

"Who's that?" she asked.

"Who's who?"

"That big black car outside the Champions'?"

Duncan slowed, and looked. As he did so, two men appeared from the house. They seem to be hurrying, but one had something wrapped round his left arm. They jumped into the car and, in just a second or two, drove down the lane far too fast, the car lurching as the driver swung it onto the road, and sped off towards Woodbury. Ruth and Duncan caught a brief sight of the man's face. It looked angry.

"There's something wrong," Ruth said.

Duncan turned into the lane and drove up to the Champions' house. He and Ruth both jumped out of the car and ran to the open door.

"Mrs Champion?"

"Peggy?" Both called out together. There was no reply. Ruth did not hesitate but ran inside. "Oh my God!" she said.

Behind her, Duncan saw Peggy Champion, lying on the floor. Ruth bent over her. Peggy's face was badly discoloured on one side. She was still breathing. Then, just inside the kitchen, Duncan saw Percy. The boy was lying in a crumpled heap. He went to see to the boy. He, too, was still breathing and, like his mother, appeared to have suffered a heavy blow to his face. He had, perhaps, fallen and hit his head. There was no other sign of injury. Ruth, her experience as an ambulance driver now coming into service, had made a very quick examination of Peggy. She had rearranged her to make her more comfortable, and she was regaining consciousness. Her eyes fluttered, and she winced with pain, trying to sit up.

"Lie still!" Ruth ordered. "Take your time. I'll get you a glass of water."

"Where's Percy?" Peggy asked, her voice croaking.

"He'll be okay," Duncan replied, but he was far from sure. He was glad that Ruth was there to help with first aid. She gave Peggy a glass of water and helped her into a chair, still unsteady, before she turned to Percy. She found a clean tea towel in the kitchen, which she dampened with cold water. Gently, she dabbed the cloth on his bruised face. It brought him round.

"Mr Frome!" Percy said, surprised.

"What happened, Percy?"

"Is Mum OK?"

"She's fine."

Reassured, Percy told them what had happened. Two men in a big car (an Austin, he said, proud that he could identify it) had knocked on the door. When Peggy opened it, they had pushed in, unasked. One of them seized her by the arm and marched her into the front room. They ignored Percy; when he tried to say something, they told him to shut up, only the exact words were too rude to repeat. They were asking his mother where the money was. She had pretended to know nothing about it. They insisted that she must have it, that it belonged to them, that Joe had stolen it from them. When she repeated it wasn't in the house, one of the men had slapped her face hard. Percy shouted to him, "The police have got it!" At that, the man who had slapped Peggy did the same again, much harder, and she fell to the floor, hitting her head as she fell. Percy, who watched from the kitchen door, grabbed a knife and went to attack the man, but the other one saw him and swung round to stop Percy, but the knife cut deeply into his arm. His mate had landed a blow which sent the boy flying. That was all he knew.

Duncan drove the two victims to hospital to get them checked over. Ruth insisted on going with them, after stopping briefly to tell a shocked Grace Cole what had happened. At the hospital they waited, but Duncan used the telephone to report the attack. Backed up by the doctor who examined the two victims, Duncan insisted that formal statements could wait until the next day. Peggy and her son were allowed to go home.

"How are you feeling, Peggy?" Ruth asked.

"Very shaky. To tell you the truth I still feel scared. What if they come back?"

"I doubt they would," Duncan said. "They'll know you'll have reported it to the police."

"I'll stay with you tonight," said Ruth. "Our house is within screaming distance." She was, Duncan acknowledged, good at defusing a situation with a weak joke.

Peggy tried to refuse, but her protest was little more than a formality.

Grace had forestalled them. By the time the four passengers arrived back at the Champions', Peggy had the place tidy and the table laid for a hot meal, which she had been preparing for Duncan and Ruth. With the addition of a few more potatoes, there was enough for all of them. It was the first time Peggy or Percy had seen such a genial party assembled in their home. The two Champions were sent off to bed soon after dark. Once the washing-up was done, Grace and Duncan returned home, but Ruth made herself as comfortable as she could in a chair. It was, she said, not the first time she had spent a night without creature comforts.

IV

Jack was confused and angry. He had lain awake most of the night after the row with his mother. He got up at first light, made himself a pot of tea, drank two cups and poured the rest into a flask. From the larder he took the cake tin and cut himself a very large slice of fruit cake. He put all this in the old army backpack, then he collected a hoe and set off for the Lower Field. It bordered The Chase.

He worked slowly, his mind turning over all the arguments of the previous evening.

The two of them had been sitting with the wireless, listening to a variety show which was not interesting to either of them. Dorothy could see that Jack had something on his mind. At last he opened the conversation.

"Why won't you tell me?" he asked. "I've got a right to know."

Dorothy put down her knitting and looked him in the eye. "No, you haven't," she said. "You do not need to know. You've got me, after all those years we've wasted. That should be enough."

"It isn't enough. Can't you see what it's like for me, not knowing who my father is?"

"I really don't know why it's so important to you. He has been out of your life, out of our lives, for nearly twenty years. What's so important about it now?"

"I don't know anybody else who doesn't know who their father is. You can see that it is driving me mad."

"I'm sure you can live with it. I can."

"I don't see why I have to live with it, as you put it. I can't even work out why you won't tell me."

Dorothy didn't answer for a moment. She was frowning/ "If it's not important to me," she said, "I can't understand why it's so important to you."

"I need to know. I need to know if I'm like him."

"Jack, I can promise you, you're nothing like him. He is, was a horrible man."

"Then... Why?"

"Why what?"

"Why did you....go with him?"

"That's my business."

"Not when I was the result, surely?"

"I don't want to talk about it."

"That's what you always say. This time I'm not going to give up until you give me an answer."

Dorothy shrugged. "You can sulk as much as you like," she said, "it won't make any difference."

"I've been looking at the jobs advertised in the Farmers Weekly."

At this Dorothy's head jerked back in shocked surprise. "What for?" she asked, but this time there was a hint of fear in her voice.

"See it from my point of view for a change. You seem to find that difficult."

"Don't talk to your mother like that!"

"I'll talk to you any way I like." Jack had worked himself into a state of real indignation. "You and Auntie Janet lied to me for sixteen years. It took you all that time to tell me I was your son. I suppose that means you are ashamed of me."

"Oh no, Jack, never say that! Of course, I'm not ashamed of you. I'm proud of you!"

"Then, how come you pretended you were my aunt, not my mother? I can't think of any other reason."

Dorothy was visibly upset now, but Jack would not allow pity for her to weaken his indignant anger.

"I tried to explain," Dorothy said, her voice now unsteady. "My own parents were very narrowminded. I couldn't even tell them I was pregnant until the bump began to show, and when I did...! To say they were furious is putting it very mildly. They more or less threw me out. I went to live with your Aunt Janet...."

"Your Aunt Janet, not mine. She's my great-aunt, remember?"

"Oh, what does that matter? She took me in. She was very kind. And, when you were born, she was happy to look after you. You were happy with her, weren't you?"

"This isn't about Aunt Janet. It's about why you didn't recognise me for sixteen years, why I was brought up, being fed a whole lot of lies. You still won't tell me who my father is."

"Jack, isn't it enough that he was a hateful man?"

"No, it's not enough. If I knew who he was, perhaps I could avoid being like him."

"I've told you, you're nothing like him."

"Who is he?"

"I'm not going to tell you."

156

"In that case, you'll have to carry on with this farm without me. There's a farm near Washington, that's looking for a farmhand.…"

"You can't! You mustn't!"

"I can, and I will. I just don't understand why it's so hard for you to tell me the truth."

But Dorothy, glimpsing what life might be like without him, began to cry. "Please don't go," she said. "I love you. You're my son. I've waited all these years to have you near me. One of these days, I know, you'll find a girl and want to marry her. That will make me sad, but it won't break my heart, what you are proposing would."

"Why won't you tell me?" Jack appeared to be unmoved by her tears.

"I can't."

"You can't? What sort of answer is that? I know about the birds and the bees. Unless you had sex with your eyes shut…"

"Jack! Jack! Don't say things like that. Don't be disgusting."

He said nothing more but stood up and turned towards the door.

"I was raped," his mother said. "He raped me. Now you know."

Jack turned as though winded. He sat down heavily and looked at his mother.

"Are you saying," he said incredulously, "that I'm the son of a rapist? Are you sure?"

"It was the one and only time," his mother admitted. She was defeated, totally dejected, afraid of the effect her admission would have on this, her only son, the son she had been obliged to watch grow up without his ever calling her mother. She had tried so hard to keep this truth from him.

"Who is this man?" He was relentless.

Now that the truth was partly out in the open, Dorothy felt something close to despair. She might have lost him already. It was probably best that he knew everything. "It was Reuben White," she said.

"The gamekeeper?"

"Yes. I wandered into The Chase. I wanted to get away from my father – I told you he was very strict. There was no laughing at home. It was mostly reading the Bible, praying, singing hymns, that sort of thing. So, I thought I'd pick some primroses to cheer up my bedroom. Reuben White saw me . I was quite pretty then, so people tell me. At first, he was quite nice to me, then he started touching me. I couldn't get away. I tried to scream but he put a hand over my mouth. I thought I was going to suffocate." Her voice wavered and her face was strained with remembered fear. "When he - finished, he watched me get up, and… And he laughed! He laughed! Can you begin to imagine what that did to me, how humiliated and helpless I felt? Can you? I felt so dirty! And there was no one I could tell, no one."

"And now he's dead." Jack stood up. He looked dazed. He made no move towards his mother, but left the kitchen, and she heard the stairs creak and the sound of his bedroom door closing. She sat and cried as though she could never stop. Finally, exhausted, she splashed water on her face at the kitchen sink, and crept wearily to her own bed, where sleep came to her rescue. She woke sometime in the middle of the night to stare into the darkness. Inside her head was an echoing darkness.

She heard Jack get up at dawn, but she did not dare confront him again. She was truly fearful that he despised her, now he knew the truth. When he left the farmhouse, she hurried downstairs to look out of the window. She saw him heading across the fields with a hoe in his hand. At least he had not left for good...yet.

Dorothy spent the day in a state of extreme anxiety. She could not guess what her son was thinking or planning. She dare not track him down to speak to him, not after the terrible argument of the previous evening, yet she longed to know. Was he still so angry that he would leave? She had no idea what effect her confession had; was he disgusted because she had admitted to being raped? For all these years she had kept the information to herself, a deep and permanent source of shame. She had done her best to forget the experience, though the memory returned unexpectedly at times and plunged her into depression. She had told only two other people, but she had never named her attacker before she told Jack. The man was dead now; that was surely an end – or was it? In confessing everything she had laid her innermost feelings bare, and she dreaded the possible consequences. To lose Jack now, when she

159

had at last been reunited with him, was unthinkable. Life would not be worth living without him. He had been the one reason she had pulled back more than once from taking her own live. She had carried on so that she could reclaim him.

She spent most of the day in the kitchen, working mindlessly on domestic chores, preparing a cottage pie, which she knew he liked. She returned to the window every five minutes, hoping and dreading to see him return. At four o'clock, exhausted, she slumped on a chair at the kitchen table with a fresh pot of tea. She did not see him as he walked across the field, and her heart leapt with fear and hope when the door opened and Jack came in. He did not bother to remove his boots. She did not care.

"Mum," he said, "I'm sorry."

She burst into tears and stood up so suddenly that the chair clattered to the floor. She took several quick steps to her son and threw her arms around him. He hugged her in return, and stroked her hair, waiting for the tears to stop.

"It's me who should be sorry," she said at last, extricating herself from his embrace, and wiping her eyes on her apron.

"Is that tea hot?" Jack asked.

She nodded and laughed, but her throat was still constricted. She poured him a cup of tea and they sat down. She was looking at him adoringly, full of hope, yet still not sure.

"I've been very selfish," he said. "There was a lot to take in, and I have been thinking so much about finding out who my father was that I forgot about you."

"I didn't want to tell you the truth," she said, "because I was so ashamed."

"Ashamed? You didn't do anything wrong. It was him." He didn't want to speak his name.

"I've been so worried all day, scared I'd lost you."

"All we've got is each other," said Jack.

It was true. It would be true until he found himself a wife. She knew that. But until then…Perhaps sharing her darkest secret was a good thing. It would be another bond, something they, and only they, shared.

"I've made you cottage pie," she said. "Why don't you have a long, hot bath while it's cooking?"

There was no need for more talk for now, but Jack, lying in the bath, had an unanswered question on his mind. What about Arthur White? He and Jack were half-brothers. He did not know Arthur, in fact, he had never spoken to him. Arthur probably had no idea he had a brother. Would it be a good idea to get to know him? Telling him they were brothers might mean giving away the secret of the rape. He couldn't do that, could he?

V

"How did you sleep?" Ruth asked.

"Not very well, to tell the truth. Too many things happening at once."

"You have had a nasty experience," Ruth commented. "Can you manage some breakfast?"

"Oh, for goodness sake! Let me do that." Ruth had made a start towards the door. Now she stopped and let Peggy prepare some food for the three of them. She was feeling quite stiff after an uncomfortable night.

They had hardly finished eating, when a police car stopped outside. Without asking permission Percy left the table and rushed to the door. Ruth raised her eyebrows; she disapproved, but she said nothing. Percy opened the door before anyone knocked. There were four policemen, two constables, the Inspector they had seen before, and another man, not in uniform. The Inspector explained, "This is Detective Superintendent Thomas," he said. "He is helping us with this case."

"Mrs Champion?" Superintendent Thomas addressed Ruth.

"No, I'm Ruth Cole, a neighbour. I've been keeping Mrs Champion company after yesterday's experience."

The Superintendent nodded. "Very sensible idea," he commented, then he turned to Peggy. "So, Mrs Champion, I wonder if you can identify the two men who assaulted you yesterday?"

"I don't think I'll ever forget them."

"That's good. That's very good. If you're feeling up to it," this man was far more sympathetic then the Inspector, Peggy thought. He sounded quite considerate. "We have a lot of pictures we would like you to look at, but it does mean another trip to Woodbury, I'm afraid."

"What, now?"

"That would be very helpful."

"Do you know what's going on?" Ruth asked.

"We have a pretty good idea. There is a gang of men, operating out of Brighton. We think they all met in the army. Some of them are particularly nasty, as I'm sure you already know. We should like to ask you a few questions, take statements now, if that's okay."

"Yes, I suppose so," Peggy was nervous.

"The first thing I would like to ask you," the Superintendent said," is, who, as well as yourself, handled the contents of that box you handed in?"

"The box? I thought you were going to ask me about yesterday."

"Oh yes, we are, but it is all connected."

"I see."

The Bear spoke; "We shall have to take your fingerprints," he said.

"Fingerprints? I'm not a criminal!"

"No, of course not." It was the Superintendent. "We need to take the fingerprints of anyone who touched the box or its contents, It's so that we can eliminate you. We hope – we believe there will be other fingerprints, especially on the money,

163

and they will be very valuable evidence. They could lead to the arrests of the members of this gang."

"Well," Peggy said hesitantly, "there was me and Grace and Mrs Dampier."

"And where do this Grace and Mrs Dampier live?" The Bear asked.

"Grace is my mother. We live just down the lane."

"What about me?" Percy wanted to get in on the act.

"You want your fingerprints taken, sonny?" the Superintendent was mildly amused. "I think we can arrange that. Constable!"

The constable in question stepped forward with a box which he placed on the table. Percy went with him, fascinated as his fingers were inked, one by one, and the tips pressed down on a special piece of paper. The policeman explained quietly, talking about whorls and loops, keeping the boy busy while the adults continued.

From Peggy they took all the details of the previous day's assault. The second constable wrote down the statement. When she described how the man who had sent Percy flying had been badly wounded with the kitchen knife, the Superintendent was frowning heavily. "Now, Percy," he said, calling him, and interrupting the fingerprinting, "Listen very carefully. It was very brave of you to try to defend your mother, but it was not a good thing to use a knife. You could have killed someone. Do you realize?"

"He deserved it." Percy was defiant. "He could have killed my mum."

"Even so, it could have been you that was being charged with murder. Never, ever, do that again. Do you understand? This is an official warning from a policeman."

There was something about this man, an authority which inspired respect even in Percy. He nodded solemnly in agreement.

Ruth described how she and Duncan had seen the two men running from the house. She was able to describe them and their car, as, indeed, was Percy.

Once the business was done, the policemen said they would be back in a short time, once they had spoken to Grace Cole and Brenda Dampier. As they were leaving, Duncan appeared. He had come, he said, just to check on Peggy and Ruth. It was time for a mid-morning cup of tea.

When the police returned, The Bear said he would send a car for Peggy, Percy, Duncan and Ruth as soon as he got back to Woodbury. Duncan said he would drive them there himself, saving the police time and trouble. Within a quarter of an hour they followed the police car.

As the Superintendent had hoped, Peggy was able to identify her attackers from the photographs. Although Percy also took part, his evidence could not be accepted, though no one informed him of that fact. The Superintendent thanked them all for their cooperation. He had been after this gang, he said, for some time. Now, especially if there were confirmatory fingerprints, he could at last proceed against them. The

165

fingerprints were important, because they were more than just the evidence of part in robberies. They also linked the attackers and Joe Champion.

As they drove home to Hartsfoot, the car was strangely silent. They were all busily trying to take in what had happened. No one voiced the question which was on all of their minds; what had all this to do with the murders in The Chase?

The Bear, however, was trying to answer that question himself. Reuben White appeared to have been connected to the Brighton gang, if only by supplying them with meat. Joe, whose 'jobs' in Brighton were now revealed as criminal, was more deeply involved perhaps. It was possible that the two men had both been shot by someone from Brighton. That, at least, seemed more likely than the alternatives. He had managed to establish some kind of motive for one or two of the inhabitants of the village, but, in each case, it was a motive concerning just one of the victims. None of them appeared to have reason to murder two men, especially if their only connection was that Reuben White was poaching his own deer. But – and this was the biggest problem – why would anyone shoot Joe Champion twice? Furthermore, who had known the whereabouts of the underground bunker, and had stolen the pistol, wiped it clean of fingerprints, and thrown it back down the shaft? Why, indeed, had he done that? It was altogether too difficult.

VI

The village was awash with rumours. The only person who had not seen the police car arrive was Martha, since it had not passed her Post Office. She had seen it on the way to the Vicarage, though she did not know exactly where it was going. It might be heading for Matthew Stevens' farm. Was that possible, she asked herself. She also asked the next two people who came in. One of them, Mrs Hale, had seen the car turn left at the end of the lane into the driveway of the Vicarage.

"Oh, my goodness!" Martha exclaimed, feigning shocked dismay, "what has been happening there?"

Mrs Hale shrugged. "It'll all come out in its own good time," she observed.

The next person added more information. "The police? Oh, they were at Peggy Champion's place earlier. They were there for hours."

Martha was better informed about the previous day's beating-up. Two men, so she understood, had arrived with crowbars, smashing down Peggy's door and ransacked her house. In the process they had knocked both the inhabitants flat and they had to be taken to hospital. The police were after them, because they were the same people that had murdered Joe Champion.

"They say," said Martha, "that Reuben White found out what Joe Champion was up to – whatever that was – and shot him, but Joe's two pals then killed Reuben. No one knows exactly what happened, and no one knows why it happened in The Chase. It's giving this village a bad name though."

Another visitor reported seeing Duncan Frome driving, Joe Champion's car out of the village, after the police had gone. What had Duncan Frome to do with all this, Martha wondered aloud. You never know what to expect when incomers come down here. He came from Liverpool somewhere, one of those big cities up north. He had probably got some underworld connections and had brought them with him. Nothing like this had happened before he came. He had started that fight with Joe Champion, right outside her shop, and then his shed had burned down – highly dangerous at a petrol station, and it was next door to her own property.

There was further reason for speculation the following day. Martha saw the familiar car, with The Bear at the wheel, as it turned down the lane next to the Post Office. It might, she thought, be going back to The Chase, but she couldn't think of a reason why. The alternative was more interesting; it could be heading for the Frost Farm. The Inspector had already been there at least once. The Frosts worked next to the wood. If anybody dared to go into The Chase while Reuben White was there, it might be one of the Frosts. But what would they want there? Was the new boy involved?

That was something The Bear was going to try to find out. His reception had been – even he attempted a little wit – quite frosty the last time. He was used to this response; it was what he usually hoped to provoke in his blundering way. There was, he was quite sure, much more to Dorothy Frost. She had been guarded when talking to him. She appeared to be afraid of something. She had reacted strangely when he asked her son about his relationship with the gamekeeper. Did she know something important, which she was keeping to herself in order to protect Jack? He was determined to find out.

Dorothy Frost did not invite him in. Instead, she told him she would not answer any more of his questions and he should leave.

"Certainly, I shall go, if that's what you want," he said, "but in that case, I'll be obliged to charge you with wasting police time and obstructing me in the course of my enquiries. I can then have you arrested and brought to the station in Woodbury, if that's what you want. Suits me, of course. I can question you there under caution. Now, what is it to be?"

Dorothy looked daggers at him, then stepped back and opened the door to the kitchen. He had arrived just as Jack was taking a break. Good, two birds with one stone. Dorothy did not ask him to sit down, but he did so anyway and, with a wave of one hand, he indicated that she should sit opposite. She did so ungraciously.

"Last time I was here," he began, "you both denied any relationship with Reuben White. I believe you were lying."

Dorothy had seldom been spoken to quite so bluntly. "Jack told you he had never even spoken to Reuben," she said.

"What about you, Mrs Frost?"

"What about me?"

"How well did you know the dead man?"

"I never spoke to him. "

169

"But you've lived here all your life, here, in Hartsfoot?"

"Yes."

"Are you telling me, that in all that time – what, fifty years or so – you didn't speak to the man who patrolled the woods at the end of your field?"

Dorothy ignored the insulting assumption that she was ten years older than she actually was. "You've seen the notice on the gate," she said. "No one goes into those words. Everybody in the village knows the story of how he has fired that shot gun of his at poachers, or at anybody else that goes into his precious woods. He was not especially liked."

"How could you like or dislike someone you didn't even know?"

"His reputation, that was enough."

This was going nowhere. He had to try something else. "What about Jack?" he said. "I suppose he didn't know much about Reuben White. After all, he only moved here a short while ago. I assume he didn't know about Mr White's reputation. Unless, of course, you told him?"

Dorothy did not reply.

"In that case, I still think you're lying. I can only deduce from what you say, what might have happened. I guess that Jack, being young and curious, ventured into the woods, met Reuben White and spoke to him, although he denies it. When White was found dead, you told Jack to keep his mouth shut."

"No!" It was Jack himself. "I told you I never spoke to the man."

"Then why did your mother look so concerned when I asked you what relationship you had with him?"

The Bear's full-on approach was working again. Jack looked decidedly rattled. He was clearly eager to defend his mother. "When you asked about a relationship," Jack said, struggling hard to express himself, "she thought you meant were our families related."

"Jack!" his mother was suddenly also agitated.

"And was there a family connection?" The Bear persisted.

"No, absolutely not!" Dorothy shouted at him." Why don't you just go away, and leave us in peace?"

"I'm going nowhere until I've got the truth, and, so far, you haven't given it to me."

"The only relationship I ever had with Reuben White was twenty years ago, when he attacked me." She was really shouting now, her eyes blazing as she leaned on the table, close enough to strike him. He had definitely found a weak point.

"When you say he attacked you," he went on, "how? Where? When exactly? Did you report it?"

"The man raped me!"

The Bear sat back in his chair. Now the truth was out, Dorothy's fury was subsiding. She was still angry, indignant and humiliated, but she was now in control.

"I did not report the incident," she said, "and it was a long time ago, nearly 20 years ago. I have had nothing whatsoever to do with Reuben White since then. Now, perhaps, you can go."

"I wish you'd told me this earlier," The Bear said. "I'm sorry you had such an experience, and I wish you had reported it all those years ago. Why on earth didn't you?"

"My parents were very, very strict. They would have blamed me. I never told them."

"Never told them?"

"No. If you had not forced me to, I wouldn't have told you, either."

"Did you know this, Jack?"

Jack licked his lips and looked nervously at his mother before he replied. "She told me the other day," he said.

"Thank you both," said The Bear, "I shall now go and leave you in peace, at least for the time being. I could charge you with wasting police time, you know. You could have told me all this the first time we spoke."

He walked out, past the barking dog, and climbed into his car. He was thinking hard. Reuben White seemed to have been a despicable man in many respects. The least of his sins was that he was stealing from his employers, killing deer, butchering them in his makeshift butchery, and selling the meat on the black market. According to his son, Arthur, he was also a brutal father, ready to use the buckle end of his belt to punish him when he was a small boy. He not only threatened trespassers on his domain, rumour had it that he would shoot at them without warning, without justification. Now, it appeared,

172

he was also a rapist! It was difficult to feel any sympathy for him, but that was not The Bear's job. Reuben White had been unlawfully killed. His murderer had to be brought to justice. In view of Dorothy Frost's revelation, both Jack and Dorothy herself, given the opportunity or, maybe, the provocation, might have wanted to take their revenge. Somehow, it did not seem likely, but it should not be entirely discounted. They had no reason to feel the same degree of animosity towards Joe Champion, however.

This, then, was another possibility, that might explain one of the murders. It was the discovery of the bullet which made any conjecture almost meaningless. Who would want to shoot the same man twice, and who had access to the bunker? He had no way of finding the answer to that question, because it was all officially secret.

VII

Graham Dampier made a muffled sound, halfway between a groan and a gasp. Brenda looked at him sharply. He staggered and fell into an armchair. He looked grey and very ill. She rushed over to him as he half-lay in the chair. His face was strangely deformed, as though paralysed on the left side. He was trying to say something, but he could only make inarticulate noises.

"Graham, what's the matter with you?" She was beginning to panic. Help, she needed help. She ran out into the hall to the telephone.

"Number please," it was the usual operator on duty.

"Emergency, please, I need an ambulance."

"Who is calling, please?"

"It's Mrs Dampier at the Vicarage in Hartsfoot. Hurry, my husband has been taken ill."

The ambulance arrived twenty minutes later. Brenda had made her husband as comfortable as she could, but he was still unable to speak. The ambulancemen came in with the stretcher, took one look at Graham, and made an immediate diagnosis: "He's had a stroke!"

The next few hours were a nightmare for Brenda. In the cottage hospital in Hazlehurst the nurses made Graham as comfortable as they could, and the doctor came along to examine him. He had lost his power of speech and, when asked to do so, was unable to raise his hands and arms as high as his shoulders.

"I'm afraid," said the doctor, "he has suffered a serious stroke."

"Is he going to get better?"

"In time he may get his speech back, but it looks as though he is paralysed down his left side. That will probably be irreversible. He is going to need a wheelchair in future."

It was devastating news. It had been so sudden. The doctor said something about a blood clot on the brain. It was a great deal to take in, and Brenda was scared; how would she cope? Where would they live? The Vicarage, their home for the past twelve years, belonged to the Diocese. Graham would be unable to continue with his work, and that would mean they would lose their home. What would they do for an income? They had some savings, but very few, certainly not enough to buy a house. Meanwhile, she would have to become a full-time nurse for her husband, something she had never even imagined. This man she had lived with for the past thirty years would now be dependent on her. He was paralysed down one side, the doctor said. That must mean that his right side was not paralysed. He would be able to do things with his right hand, surely. Would he be able to write? He couldn't talk at the moment, but would he be able to write things down? He seemed to understand what the doctor said to him at least.

The news spread rapidly through the village. Everyone was shocked. The regular churchgoers were dismayed. They sent Get Well cards to the hospital. Graham, propped up in the bed, smiled crookedly on one side of his face. It was more like a grimace than a smile, but, when Brenda read the words and the signatures to him, he obviously understood.

She telephoned the Bishop. He was understanding, sympathetic, practical. He knew of Brenda's work before she had met Graham. She was working in the Diocesan Office, where she was Diocesan Secretary, when young Graham, newly ordained, had visited the Bishop. There was an immediate, mutual attraction. It led to their marriage the following year, when Graham had been appointed to the living in Hartsfoot.

Brenda had left her job. The present incumbent was helpful now she faced a difficult time. He would arrange for a curate to come and take over the regular services. In return Brenda agreed to accommodate the new man. She asked about the tenancy of the Vicarage. The Bishop told her not to worry about it for the moment, but to concentrate on helping her husband recuperate as far as possible. As for her financial concerns, she should not worry about them for the time being: he would explore possible funds to help her, when it became necessary.

It was, thought Brenda, almost like dealing with a death. There were so many people to notify, so many things to arrange. Fortunately, Brenda had always been the one who dealt with financial matters, experience which gave her a full understanding of their immediate problems. She would need to acquire a wheelchair. She found one, second-hand, and brought it home in the back of the car in which Duncan Frome had kindly ferried her around. Once back at the Vicarage, she discovered it was too wide to go through the doorways. It was going to be a very difficult time ahead. She wondered how Graham was going to keep clean, since he would be unable to get in and out of the bath, even if she were to help him. The whole thing was almost too much for her, but friends proved very kind and supportive. It was at such times, she realized, that you discovered who your friends really were. It never crossed her mind that the kindness she received was an enthusiastic return on all she had done over the years for the village.

A complication she had not even thought of, but which occurred to Duncan Frome, was that Graham would no longer be able to serve on the Parish Council. Once again, the possibility loomed that the Council might collapse and be taken over by the District Council, based in Hazlehurst. It was of no particular concern to Brenda, but to the four remaining Councillors it was cause for concern. They held an emergency meeting. After agreeing to send a formal card to the Vicar, wishing him a speedy recovery, they discussed what they should do. None of them had any idea of likely recruits to the Council.

"Why don't we hold an open meeting in the Village Hall?" Duncan suggested. "That way we can point out the choice facing the village. It might be enough to persuade at least one person to join us. It would be even better if we could recruit two or three new faces."

The suggestion was treated sceptically at first, but, after twenty minutes' discussion, the other three Councillors agreed. It would be a good opportunity, Matthew Stevens suggested, to get the Police Inspector in to explain what was going on about the murder investigation. People were still uneasy. The murderer had not been arrested. Did the police know who it was? The farmer's suggestion was seen as a very good way to get more people to attend. They would come to learn about the police investigation, but it would also be a chance to recruit at least one new Councillor. Several notices were set up in the village, including one in the Post Office, and the meeting was advertised by word-of-mouth. Each of the Councillors made a point of mentioning it to everybody they met. The meeting would take place at 7:30 on Wednesday evening.

The Bear agreed to address the meeting. The Hall was surprisingly full: as John Stevens had supposed, the villagers were especially interested in what progress the police had made in identifying the murderer of Rueben White and Joe Champion. There were as many women as men in the Hall.

Mervyn Hardcastle had agreed to chair the meeting. With characteristic thoroughness he had brought a wooden gavel. Under his direction they set up a table on the small stage. The four Councillors would sit behind it. The Inspector would be introduced, and he would talk to the assembled villagers and answer their questions. After that, Mervyn planned to ask for volunteers to serve on the Council.

As the Hall began to fill, Mervyn Hardcastle and Duncan Frome felt some concern, as they recognised a group of six or seven men. They had obviously been drinking; there was a noticeable smell of beer about them, and Duncan thought he had seen at least one or two of them in the past, drinking in the Horse and Hounds. They were, he believed, friends of Joe Champion. He assumed they had come because they wanted information about the search for Joe's killer.

The meeting began in an orderly fashion. Mervyn Hardcastle introduced the Inspector, and The Bear began to sketch out what little progress had so far been made. He made no reference to the use of a pistol, leaving the impression that both Joe and the gamekeeper had been killed with the same shot gun. He explained the impossibility of their having shot one another, and the fact that there must, therefore, be a third person involved.

"Who is this third person, then?" one of Joe's friends shouted from the back of the hall, interrupting The Bear in full flow.

"We don't know that yet," he said.

"That's not good enough," another man shouted." You're useless!"

This brought a murmur of disapproval from other people in the Hall, and Mervyn Hardcastle tried to reprimand the speaker. "I'm sure the police are doing their best," he said. "We aren't here to challenge them, just to get the facts."

"They don't know what the facts are!"

"If you know anything, you should come and tell us about it." The Bear told the man.

"You haven't a clue, you lot. You don't even know who murdered these two. How are we supposed to have any faith in you? There's people in the village as had it in for Joe, you know."

"Are you accusing someone? You'd better be careful what you say."

But the protester was not going to be silenced easily."Hartsfoot was a quiet little place before certain outsiders moved in. I'll say no more."

There was an audible gasp all round. It was obvious the man was referring to Duncan Frome.

The Bear warned the man again. If he had hard evidence, he should take it to the police. But the damage had been done, there had always been some villages who mistrusted Duncan as an outsider. They had added fuel to their own flames when he had rebuilt the bicycles and made a profit. They firmly believed that he it was who had attacked Joe Champion. As for the burning down of his hut, he had probably done that, they reckoned, in order to claim the insurance. Most of all, they didn't like the way he talked, that funny accent he had, the whining way in which his voice was used. Now their prejudice was given free rein and there was much indignant chatter.

Mervyn Hardcastle banged his gavel and The Bear held up a large hand, as though he were stopping traffic. "You all now know as much as we do," he lied. "If any of you has any real, hard evidence, it is your duty to come and tell us, the police." And with that he turned, bade a brief farewell to Mervyn, and strode out of the Hall.

Mervyn banged the gavel again. "Perhaps I should remind you," he said, "I am one of the newcomers that Frank Thompson refers to. I hope he is not suggesting I am connected with the murder of Joe Champion and Reuben White. Perhaps you don't know, but I am a member of the syndicate that owns the Estate, so Reuben White was, technically, my employee."

"If I may speak," a female voice could be heard above the murmured responses in the audience; it was Ruth Cole. "I am ashamed of this village," she said, "I was born here, and lived here most of my life. I've seen what Mr Hardcastle has done, what he has given to this village. Would any of you here have organised the grass cutting, got the pavements properly maintained, even provided a cricket pitch for us? No!" She answered her own question. "And Mr Frome? He has taken over an abandoned plot that has been an eyesore for years. He is planning to turn it into a well-designed, modern garage which will bring trade and visitors." She stopped. She had the attention of the audience. Most of them were unaccustomed to hearing a woman speak out in this way, almost like a politician, ready to challenge them.

Mervyn Hardcastle thanked her briefly, and quickly raised the subject of the Vicar's stroke. The mood changed. Most of the audience were sympathetic. He explained that the Parish Council would collapse, unless they could find volunteers to serve, "Even though it means serving alongside two incomers," he said.

There were no volunteers. He brought the meeting to a close and people left amid the clatter of chairs and talk. It had not been what the four Councillors had hoped. However, two men approached Mervyn, one was George, the publican, the other was Ed Simpson, a quiet man who worked for the Estate as a painter and decorator. They were both offering their services.

VIII

Duncan did not hear the boy. He chanced to look up and saw him, standing uncertainly just inside the door. He was very pale, his face taut.

"Percy!" Duncan said, standing up, away from the bench, "is something the matter? Your mum?"

The boy said nothing, but he shook his head. He was the picture of misery.

"Well, come in, then, if you're going to."

But Percy remained on the threshold of the Old Forge. He was holding the doorpost and shifting uneasily from foot to foot. Duncan frowned. He could not understand what was wrong.

"It was me," the boy said.

"What was you? What are you talking about?"

Percy blurted, "I set light to your shed."

"You?" Duncan was profoundly shocked. He thought Percy had become a friend. This was awful news. "Why?" he asked.

"Dad made me. He said he'd kill me if I didn't do it."

"I still don't know why. Why didn't he do it himself?"

Percy was crying now. "He said he'd be iin the pub so everyone would know it wasn't him. You won't hit me, will you, Mr Frome? I know you won't want ever to see me again. I'm sorry I burned your shed down.." He turned and started to walk away, still crying.

"Percy, come back! You're not going anywhere until you've made us both a pot of tea. You can see my hands are dirty."

"You mean it? You aren't going to give me a good hiding?"

"Of course, I mean it. Now, dry your eyes and make that tea. It took guts for you to tell me."

Percy wiped his eyes on his sleeve."Mum said I had to," he said.

"You should listen to your mum. She'll only give you good advice, not like your dad."

"I thought you'd never want to see me again."

"I haven't wasted all these months getting your reading up to scratch to lose track of your progress now. I want you to go on coming here, and I want you to promise me that from now on you are going to do your best at school."

"But Miss Proctor.."

"Whatever you think about your teacher, you should try to learn. She might surprise you, if you show her you are really trying."

Percy looked doubtful. "Why do you care what I do at school?" he asked.

Duncan watched him as he made tea. He was a capable lad, handling a kettle of boiling water with care. He carried the teapot over to the bench and put it down. He still looked nervous.

"What's done is done," Duncan said. "I'm going to tell you something very few other people in the village know about me."

Percy looked at him, startled.

"I used to be married," Duncan told him."We lived in Coventry, a big city. I worked in a factory that made motorcycles."

"What happened?"

"I was in the army, and while I was away, a German bomber dropped a bomb on the house. My wife and my parents were in the house. They were all killed."

Percy didn't know how to respond to this confidence. He said nothing.

"When I first met you, you looked like you were going to waste your opportunities. I didn't want that to happen. Life's too precious to waste it. You should make the most of it."

"Even if you have to work at something you don't like, like English or geography?"

"Exactly. Now, I'm prepared to trust you. Will you listen to my advice?"

"It's hard," Percy observed.

"Yes, it is, sometimes, but it's worth it in the end."

"I wish you were my dad."

Duncan was truly touched at this, but said nothing, he drained his mug and stood up. "Is your mum all right?" he asked. "She's not still scared those men will come back, is she? They're safely locked up now."

"She says she's OK, but I think she's still worried."

"Well, you'll just have to look after her."

"I like Miss Cole," Percy said.

"Ruth? Yes, she's very nice, isn't she?"

"Is she going to stay here now?"

"I don't know."

The conversation was interrupted, as Duncan caught sight of an army lorry coming from the direction of Woodbury.

It was a three-tonner with a canvas tilt on the back, but what made him stare was the bright red board in front of the radiator. On it were the words, Bomb Disposal Unit, and the truck was slowing to turn past the Post Office. It was followed by two, smaller vehicles in the same, khaki livery.

"Bomb Disposal?" Duncan spoke out loud. "Where can they be going?"

Martha Brewer in the Post Office was asking the same question. Unfortunately, there was no one to answer her. Although she was immensely proud of her position as Postmistress, especially since it gave her access to all kinds of information, she had grown increasingly frustrated over the past few weeks at being confined to one place. So many interesting things had been happening, many of them not only out of her line of sight, but where others had seen them first. The sight of the army lorry with the clear "Bomb Disposal Unit" sign, was a cause of great curiosity to her, but she could not leave the Post Office to find out more for herself. She decided on a partial solution. She picked up the telephone and asked the operator, Sylvia, to put us through to the offices of the Hazlehurst and District Times. It was, she knew, only a second-best solution; Sylvia would undoubtedly be listening in, and the up substance of the conversation would soon be known in the entire district.

She asked to speak to a reporter. There was only one, junior reporter, by the name of Bert Price. He was no more than a boy of seventeen, who expected to spend his time in the local, Magistrates Court, or at school prize-giving is and the occasional wedding. His biggest assignment of this year had been to witness the Boxing Day Meet of the local Hunt. Informed by Martha that there was an unexploded gone in

185

Hartsfoot, he was very excited. He grabbed a small notebook and pencil, and positively ran out of the office to his small, two-stroke motorbike. It was his pride and joy, and it started at the third kick in a cloud of blue smoke. He arrived at the Hartsfoot Post Office twenty minutes later.

"Where's the bomb?" he asked.

"Before I tell you, promise me something." If he had known the word, he would have described this response as prevarication.

"What do you want?"

"I want you to promise to call in here on your way back to the office. After all, I'm the one who put you onto this story. It's only right you should keep me informed."

Bert gave her a surprised look, but said, "OK."

"They went down this lane." Martha pointed. "Unless they've stopped at the bottom, by the brook, it only leads to the Frost farm. I don't remember hearing about the bomb being dropped there."

"If it didn't explode…"

"We'd have heard the plane."

"OK," he said again, and left.

He passed the point where the brook ran under the road in a conduit without seeing any sign of the Bomb Disposal Unit, so he continued up the track towards the farm. Then he saw the army truck. It was parked at the entrance to the woods in front of him. He dismounted. There was one man in uniform, a corporal. He was busy with a hammer and nails, attaching a large notice to the gate. It read, "Danger! Unexploded Bomb. Do Not Pass This Notice."

Bert approached the corporal. "Press!" he announced.

The corporal suppressed a grin and the impulse to reply, "Press what?" Instead, he simply looked at Bert and waited.

"Where is this bomb?"

"No idea, sir." The "Sir" was very slightly over-accentuated.

"But you were here to, well, to dispose of it, aren't you?"

"Not me, sir. I'm just the driver."

"So, it's in the woods somewhere, is it?"

"I suppose it must be, sir. I can't tell you anything. You would need to speak to the Major."

"Can I speak to him, then?"

"I imagine he's busy at the moment, taking the thing to pieces. And I can't let you past in any case."

"I'll wait."

"Your choice. It could be a long wait, though. I have known these things take as much as two days. It depends on the bomb, you see, it's condition as well as its type."

"Two days!"

"Could be. Could be five or six hours. Can't tell. If you want my advice, sir," again, the hint of insolence, "I'd to go and find myself a nice cup of tea somewhere in the village. You will hear the bang when it goes off."

"When it goes off?"

"Oh yes, sir, they're bound to blow it up here. It's much easier than trying to take it back to the depot. They'll have to build a wall of sandbags or something to keep the blast in. That all takes time, even if defusing the thing is difficult."

Bert was in a quandary. This was a big story for him, but he couldn't wait five or six hours, or even two days. There wasn't even any one he could ask for a comment, so he could quote them, as he had been told he should. The driver had climbed back into his cab, leaving the door open. He was watching Bert, waiting for him to decide to go. Meanwhile, he watched him with mild smile on his face and smoked a cigarette. After ten minutes of indecision, Bert got back on his motorcycle and headed back as far as the Post Office. He bought himself a bottle of Tizer.

"Well?" Martha asked.

"It's a big bomb," Bert reported inventively. "It's going to take a long time, but they are going to blow it up in the woods."

"In The Chase? What's it doing there? I lived here right through the war, and we never had any bombs dropped, exploded or unexploded."

"If it didn't explode," Bert reasoned, "you wouldn't have heard it, would you?"

"We'd have heard the aeroplane."

That seemed a reasonable thing to say. How did the bomb get there, if there had been no enemy aircraft? Perhaps, thought Bert, this might yet turn into a good story. He put the stopper back into the Tizer bottle and snapped the spring fastening. He had the beginnings of a story, at least. His bike started again first time. He sped off back to the office.

Had Bert waited an hour, he would have heard the explosion, as did everyone in the village. It was remarkably subdued for a big bomb, and it sounded more like a heavy thump than a bang. It was a very heavy thump which produced vibrations, a little like an earth tremor. Everyone heard or felt it, and was mystified; why had it not been a bigger bang? But it was the very existence of a bomb which was the main talking point. No one had heard of any bombs being dropped on or near Hartsfoot. That was a mystery in itself.

The village policeman, PC Mallow, was also mystified. He thought it worth reporting to his superiors. It occurred to him that the explosion in The Chase might destroy evidence in the murder case. It would do no harm to report to the Inspector in charge. It might help to restore some confidence in him as a policeman, since the Inspector had made it plain he thought him incompetent. That stung.

The Bear was, indeed, interested. He spoke to his own boss, the Super, and he, in turn, phoned the Bomb Disposal Squad. They gave him evasive answers, but, in the end, there came a phone call from the Security Officer, Mr Jones.

"The security of the Unit had been blown," he stated. "Someone obviously knows about the bunker in your woods, so the decision was made to destroy it completely."

"There was no bomb?"

"No. That's a simple cover story."

The Bear was furious. Without so much as a by-your-leave the decision had been taken to destroy evidence. True, it was evidence he had been told would not be allowed, but it was evidence, and, if all else failed, a good lawyer might have been able to use it. He wondered if there had been any other evidence, which they had missed, but which would now be for ever compromised.

The next day he revisited The Chase, ignoring the warning signs which had been left there. He walked past the place where the heads and feet of the slaughtered deer had been found and made his way to the site of the bunker. There was a deep hollow, but to the casual eye there was no sign of a bunker; the soldiers had done a very good job of concealing it. No bits of concrete could be seen. A couple of trees had fallen across the site itself, but quantities of soil, twigs and dead leaves had been thrown over the ground where the entrance to the bunker had been. The Bear looked around for fifty yards but found nothing, except, in a small space between two trees he spotted a freshly broken branch. Looking closer, he found a cast iron disk, the lid of the bunker. It had been blown by the force of the explosion high in the air to land thirty yards from its original position.

IX

"It's your eighteenth birthday this week," said Dorothy. "What would you like to do?"

Jack looked at her. What he really wanted, but a new was impossible, was to have a car of his own. Other than that, he had no idea.

"It is a special occasion," Dorothy continued. "I wish we could afford to do something really grand."

"I'm not bothered," Jack said. "There is one thing I would quite like to do."

"What's that?"

"Just to celebrate, I'd like to go to the pub and have a beer."

Dorothy was taken aback. She came of a teetotal family and had never set foot in a pub in her life. The very thought of doing so filled her with alarm. "Do you think that's a good idea?" she asked.

"But the people I know celebrate that way. I don't want to get drunk or anything."

Dorothy was too happy to be reunited with him after all these years to argue over such a minor point. Jack's birthdays brought with them as much pain as pleasure, reminding her, as they did, of the ugly way in which he had been conceived. She loved him dearly as an individual, and she had tried all these years to dismiss thoughts of his father as of no consequence. There was still a niggling fear that he would bring up the subject of his half-brother, by all accounts a worthless young man, and one she would prefer him to have no connection with.

Jack's birthday fell on a Saturday. She fell in with his wishes but drew the line at going into a public house with him. Instead, she drove him into Hazlehurst, where he met two young men from Belham, who had been to school with him, and joined them for 'a quiet drink' in the Rising Sun, while Dorothy went to the local cinema. They arranged to meet at the end of the film, when she would drive him home.

The evening went as planned, though Jack, unused to drinking alcohol, grew quite tipsy by the end of the evening. His mother controlled her natural disapproval, merely asking him if he had had a nice time. She hated the smell of beer on his breath, and was very glad to get back to the farm. Jack was unusually talkative, but Dorothy did not take in anything he said. She made a hot drink and was in a hurry to get to bed.

X

"Yes, Mrs Clements?" Mervyn Hardcastle looked up as his housekeeper knocked on the door of the sitting room and came in.

"Sorry to disturb you, sir, but there is an Inspector Blundell to see you."

Mervyn swallowed his annoyance. "Show him in, Mrs Clements."

The Bear was ushered in. He did not look particularly unsure of himself after the last encounter with Hardcastle, who did not invite him to sit down. Instead, he barked, "Well?"

"I'm sorry to disturb you, sir," The Bear lied cheerfully. "But this is a matter of urgency, as I'm sure you'll agree."

"I hope this has nothing to do with the matter we discussed last time."

"Only indirectly, sir."

"Well, what is it?"

"In the course of our investigation," The Bear began, bu he was interrupted by an impatient gesture from the little man.. There was nothing in the least Pickwickian about him this time.

"Spare me the jargon," he said. "Just spit it out."

"As I was saying, sir, in the course of our investigation into the murders in The Chase, we had reason to make a thorough search of the area. We discovered a patch of ground which appeared to have been disturbed, so I ordered my officers to dig it."

"I trust you are not going to tell me they disinterred more bodies." The tone was sarcastic.

"Not exactly, sir. We unearthed the remains of six deer."

"Six deer?"

"Yes, sir, only the heads and feet. It would appear they had been slaughtered for their meat, but heads and feet have no value in that sense."

193

"Very strange, Inspector, but what is your point?"

"The gamekeeper, Reuben White, sir, has been poaching his own deer, it seems, and selling the meat on the black market."

"Are you sure of this? It is a serious allegation."

"We have all kinds of evidence and statements, sir. The venison was taken to Brighton, where it was used in various hotels and restaurants."

"I see." Hardcastle was clearly taken aback by this news. "And why, exactly, do you feel it necessary to inform me about this, Inspector? The man you should talk to is the Estate Manager, Jim Scrivener, at the Estate Office in Hazlehurst."

The Bear coughed, as if to delay the delivery of a delicate response. "I'm sorry to say, sir, that Scrivener was well aware of the theft."

"What?" This was like an explosion of disbelief.

"We have had to requisition his accounts, sir. I believe Scrivener has been systematically skimming off money for himself. I believe you are one of the Directors of the Syndicate that owns the Estate. That is so, is it, sir?

"Yes, I am a Director. There are four others.I think you had better sit down, Inspector, and give me the details. I could do with a cup of coffee."

Mervyn Hardcastle was thinking furiously. His co-Directors lived some way away. They would be understandably concerned at this news. The day to day running of the Estate was delegated to the Manager. Without a Manager in post – and

Scrivener would obviously have to go – someone would have to take charge. It looked very much as though Hardcastle would have to cope, until a new man could be recruited. It was not something he wanted to do. He had retired happily into this village and enjoyed being no longer concerned with routine business matters. Perhaps he had been too remote and had neglected the proper oversight of the Estate. Board meetings, held twice a year, were hardly serious affairs, more like pleasant parties for the five, elderly partners. They had invested a lot of money in the Estate, however, and they should have been more watchful.

"Tell me more about this venison business," he said.

The Bear described the butcher's workshop attached to Reuben White's cottage.

"You believe Scriverner was aware of this business?"

"It seems likely. Anyone who visited the cottage could have discovered it."

"Six deer, you say?"

"We found six heads and the remains of the feet, but there may well have been others. There were two carcases hanging on hooks in White's shed."

"Quite a serious amount of livestock."

"Yes, sir."

Hardcastle sipped his coffee. "Well, thank you for informing me," he said. "You can leave it with me, now, Inspector."

"Well, sir," said The Bear, "of course you must organize Scrivener's replacement, and I'm happy for you to inform your co-Directors , but Scrivener will be charged with fraud, and our Fraud Office will be investigating the accounts."

"Is that necessary, Inspector?"

"It's not for me to decide, sir. A crime has been committed – several crimes, if you take in the embezzlement, theft of the deer, the illegal selling of the meat, and that has nothing much to do with the murder of Reuben White. At least, not so far as we know as yet."

When the Inspector left, Hardcastle sat for a while and began to plan, then he picked up the phone and began talking.

XI

It would be good, Duncan thought, when the new building was completed, and he had a proper office to work in. He had managed surprisingly well with this makeshift desk at one end of the Forge, but a custom-built office in a spanking, new building which would one day be a proper showroom, that was definitely a step forward. He was feeling more and more positive about the future these days. The war was behind him, as was the first part of his life. His marriage had been wonderful, and the loss, whenever he allowed himself to think about it, was still deeply painful, but Audrey would have been proud of him for looking forwards rather than dwelling on the past. A fresh start, that is what he had planned, and it was proving rewarding as well as challenging.

"Hallo." The familiar voice broke into his reflections. Ruth had come into the Forge. He stood up.

"Kind of you to grace us with your presence," he said.

"I've come to say yes, if it's for a trial period."

At first, he did not understand.

"The apprenticeship," she said. She looked at him, mouth half open, a tiny crease in her forehead showing she was unsure of the answer. He did not reply, but he stepped forward and took her in his arms and kissed her. He let her go and stepped back.

"I'm so sorry," he said, as surprised by his own action as she was.

"Don't apologise," she said. "That was lovely. I imagine it means yes."

"Yes, of course, yes. But I shouldn't..."

"Duncan," she said, "I said don't apologise. I don't imagine I shall get that kind of treatment every time I turn up for work, though."

He laughed, but he was feeling confused. Until this moment he had not thought of Ruth other than as a friend. Things seemed to be changing fast.

A car pulled up outside the door. It was Mervyn Hardcastle. He stepped out of the vehicle and walked into the Forge, raised his hat to Ruth, and addressed Duncan.

"How soon will the building work be done?" he asked.

"The extension to the Forge itself should be competed in a couple of weeks at the latest. Why do you ask?"

"I may have a business proposition for you."

"Oh?"

"I have been obliged to sack the Estate Manager," Mervyn announced. "I won't bore you with the details, but for the present I am more or less obliged to take on much of the work he should be doing."

"I thought you were happily retired."

"That's what I thought, too. However, it appears that he had been doing some very shady business. One of the contracts Scrivener arranged was for the servicing of the Estate's vehicles. There aren't all that many, but I will want to negotiate a new deal for myself. If you can assure me you can cope with the numbers, and regularity of servicing..."

"How many, and what kind of vehicles?"

Duncan explained that Ruth would be working with him, but he did not explain it would be as an apprentice, giving the impression that she had plenty of experience. She remained an interested listener.

Mervyn asked to see the books, and he wanted to know what the new buildings would be like. He was especially concerned with the capacity to deal with the regular work. Duncan did all he could to reassure him there would be no problem.

The discussion lasted an hour. Mervyn said he would prefer the business to be handled in Hartsfoot, if at all possible, taking it back from Hazlehurst; it was the village he had made his own. He would get his solicitors working on a draft contract.

When he had left, Duncan's head was whirling. It seemed the murder of the gamekeeper had led to the discovery of fraud, and that in turn had offered him, Duncan, the break he needed. Still quite dazed, he fumbled with a kettle to make a pot of tea. He turned from the fire and found himself smiling broadly at Ruth.

"You seem to be bringing me luck," he said.

She didn't answer but kissed him. "You deserve some luck," she said. "It's about time. And you're going to need all the help you can get. You really need a properly qualified mechanic, not me."

"Don't say that," he said. "We can make this work between us."

Exactly what he meant by this, neither of them knew for certain, but they didn't bother to analyse it.

XII

Dorothy Frost was already in a sour mood when she opened the door on Monday morning. She had been dismayed when Jack had emerged from the Rising Sun a little the worse for wear. He was not so drunk as to be unsteady on his feet, or incapable, but alcohol had certainly affected him, and he had been unusually talkative. She had lain awake on Saturday night for hours, hearing him snoring in the adjoining bedroom. She hoped he was not developing an early taste for alcohol. Her views on drinking had been almost entirely formed by her strict upbringing, not from any personal experience. She had been brought up to believe that it was sinful even to enter a public house, and that drink was indeed the curse of the working man. She had no way of assessing Jack's behaviour, other than to worry about it. As for Jack himself, he had spent most of Sunday feeling physically unwell. He was also acutely aware of his mother's disapproval, which did little to alleviate the headache. He and his mother said very little to one another on Sunday. He had mumbled some excuse after lunch, which, uncharacteristically, he only pecked at, and had taken himself out for a walk. On impulse he decided to explore The Chase for the first time. He found the solitude and silence, broken only by birdsong, more relaxing. He had found a fallen tree to sit on for an hour, while he smoked and hoped that his head would feel better soon.

So, Dorothy was on her own at 9:30 in the morning; Jack was working in the fields. The last person Dorothy wanted to see was The Bear. He raised his hat and asked if he could come in.

"What is it this time?" Dorothy asked. "Unless you have something important to say, I'm not sure that I want to speak to you."

"I told you the last time I was here," he said, "that I would have to come back with more questions. If you really don't want to speak to me here, I can always insist that you come to Woodbury. We can conduct a formal interview there, if you so wish."

Dorothy stood back and allowed him into the kitchen, where, uninvited, he pulled out a chair and sat at the table. He put his hat on the table and waited for her to take her place opposite him.

"Well, Inspector?"

"I shall need to speak to Jack as well, I'm afraid."

"He's working."

"I assumed he would be. Can you possibly ask him to come in?"

Dorothy heaved an expressive and reluctant sigh. "It will take me five minutes to fetch him," she said.

"In that case, I wonder if you would be kind enough to offer me a cup of tea?"

Dorothy gave him an astonished stare, hardly believing his audacity, but she walked over to the range to pick up the kettle. She put tea into a teapot and made the tea without another word. She put the pots down on the table with a thump, fetched a large cup and saucer, a bowl of sugar, and a jug of milk, put them down noisily in front of him, and left in search of her son. The Bear smiled and poured himself a cup.

Mother and son reappeared as he was pouring himself his second cup of tea. They joined him at the table.

"What I wanted to ask both of you," The Bear said, "is something quite simple: you are the people who live closest to The Chase. We have no witnesses who can give us any information about people's coming and going. An important hope is that one or other of you may have seen someone either entering or leaving the woods. Even if it wasn't on the day of the murders, it could prove helpful." He stopped and looked at each of them quizzically. They both looked strained, humourless. Neither replied.

"You must have seen people going into the woods, however occasionally," he said.

"I don't remember ever seeing anyone at all," Dorothy said.

"And you, Jack?"

The young man shook his head. "Only me," he said. Dorothy looked at him sharply, "When did you…?"

"Yesterday," he said.

"And before that?" asked The Bear.

"What do you mean?"

"Was yesterday the first time you went into the woods?"

"Yes."

"You are quite sure?"

"Jack is not a liar!" Dorothy was quick to defend her son.

"While I was sitting here," The Bear remarked, "I couldn't help noticing the two tins of corned beef." He nodded towards the top of a cupboard.

"What about them?" Dorothy was clearly surprised by his question.

"Can I ask how you acquired them?"

"Is that any of your business?"

"Yes, it is, you see, Mrs Frost, my job as a policeman is to be inquisitive. When I saw those tins, I felt I had to look at them more closely. They are not your usual tins of corned beef."

"What do you mean by that?"

"On the bottom of each tin, if you look, you'll see what I mean."

Dorothy was both annoyed and puzzled. She fetched a tin and turned it over. "Oh!" she exclaimed, then, turning to her son, "Where did you get these, Jack?"

"So, it was you? Yes, where did you get them? This is very important, so you'd better tell me the truth."

"I bought them."

"Where?"

"It was a bloke in the pub. He said they were Army Surplus. I paid good money for them, two and six each."

"Tell me more." The Bear sounded faintly sceptical.

"It was my eighteenth birthday on Saturday," Jack explained. "Mum drove us into Hazlehurst and I met a couple of mates and went for a drink."

"I shall need their names."

"What do you need their names for?" Dorothy asked.

"Just routine, Mrs Frost. We need to confirm the story."

"It's not a story! Jack doesn't lie!"

"I'm sure you're right, but I'll still need names."

Jackie gave him the names of the two friends and told him where they lived in Belham.

"And who was the person who sold you these tins?"

"I don't know. I've never seen him before."

"First things first," The Bear was trying to be patient. "What was the name of the pub?"

"The Rising Sun."

"I know it. It hasn't got a very good reputation."

"First time I'd been there."

"Probably not the best pub for your first drink – I take it was your first drink?"

Jack nodded dumbly. It was bad enough that his mother disapproved, without this bullying policeman.

"And what about this man who sold you the bully beef?"

"Dark-haired bloke called Arthur, I think it was."

"Arthur what?"

"I don't know. He didn't say."

"Well, if what you say is true,…"

"Of course, it's true!" Dorothy was defending her son once more and sounding quite stressed.

"I'm afraid I have to confiscate these two tins," The Bear said. "They are almost certainly stolen goods, so I could, in theory at least, charge you with handling stolen goods."

"Jack! How could you be so stupid?" Dorothy was at the end of her tether.

The Bear shrugged, reached for his hat, which he crammed on his head, gathered both tins, and turned towards the door. "I suggest you steer well clear of The Rising Sun," he said. "I shan't charge you with any offence this time. I'm afraid you've lost five bob. I'll let myself out."

XIII

"Oh, my dear Lord!" Grace put down the receiver. She looked shocked.

"What's happened?" Ruth asked.

They had all three been sitting quietly, listening to the wireless, when the phone rang. Grace, who had been expecting a call from Emily, had answered the phone. Ruth and Duncan assumed from her reaction that this was bad news from Coventry.

"It's the Vicar," she said. "He had a second stroke. He didn't survive. Poor Brenda!"

The first reaction was consternation. It had been so sudden. The first stroke had been serious, but none of them had considered the possibility of a second. The Vicar had been a pillar of strength during the war. He had been constantly cheerful, at least until recently, providing support and comfort to his parishioners, and Brenda had shared the load as far as she could. Church attendance had been quite good, though the younger generation were less regular in their attendance. Attendance in general had been good, however, no doubt partly because the war was taking its toll. People were anxious, sometimes afraid, often worried about the missing menfolk. Times were uncertain, and there had been times, when the threat of invasion hung over them like a dark cloud. It was at such times that Graham Dampier had proved his worth. He had kept their spirits up, encourage them to have faith. Now, suddenly, he had gone.

Grace and her daughter had known the Vicar for twelve years. Duncan, on the other hand, had only known him for a short time, and that was largely because he had served with him on the Parish Council. He had respected the man, but for Ruth and Grace it was a different relationship. Grace in particular felt it keenly. She was distressed at the news. Duncan took it upon himself to go and make a cup of tea, leaving the two women to reminisce and come to terms with yet another loss.

Brenda was reeling with the shock. The stroke had been a very unpleasant shock to the system, but at no point had she thought in terms of losing her husband completely. It would, she knew, take a long time to come to terms with widowhood. Her sister, Patricia, lived in Kent with her husband and three children. She was not y in a position to come and help, and Brenda could not leave Hartsfoot. She would have to make the funeral arrangements and deal with all the business, business which she had dealt with on behalf of many other parishioners over the years. She had, what is more, already agreed to look after the new curate, a young man called Peter Hanlon. When Grace Cole offered to keep her company, therefore, she had accepted, but she had a few reservations. Grace was not intrusive by nature, but Brenda was far from sure she needed anybody around her until she had taken in the enormity of Graham's death.

Since it was already getting dark, Duncan and Ruth walked with Grace as far as the Vicarage. They left her there and walked back. If asked, she said, she would stay the night with Brenda. If not, she would ring up, so that one of them could walk back with her.

Duncan and Ruth walked back down the village street. The village was largely deserted. There were lights in the windows.

"Another death!" Ruth said sadly. "This has been a terrible year."

"There have certainly been plenty of unpleasant surprises," Duncan agreed.

"This place has changed out of all recognition. It is no longer the village I grew up in."

They walked on in companionable silence. Perhaps things were changing too rapidly, Duncan reflected. He was himself part of those changes. But there had been others: two men had been killed, that seemed to be the beginnings of it all. Dorothy Frost's father had died, and suddenly she had produced a grown-up son, Jack, a newcomer to Hartsfoot. Joe Champion, murdered, had been revealed as a thief. Reuben White had been killed too, and he had been involved in serious theft, possibly in fraud. The Estate Manager had also been involved in crime and had now been sacked. Mervyn Hardcastle was left with the difficult job of reorganising and administering the Estate, when he only wanted to enjoy his retirement. Ruth had lost her job in Luton, but that, he hoped, was not such a bad thing, since it had led her to work with him. Furthermore, very much to his surprise, he had feelings for her which he thought would have been impossible. One of the biggest changes in the village was the development of his own business. Now that he had a very good chance of a regular contract with the Estate, it was set to grow.

"We have to accept change, it's part of life," he said. "And sometimes change can be a good thing. I'm very glad you are here."

By way of reply Ruth squeezed his hand and pressed close to him as they neared home.

The phone rang at about eleven o'clock. Ruth answered it.

"Brenda would like me to stay the night," Grace said. "I'll see you in the morning."

She and Brenda sat in the dark, Victorian sitting room at the Vicarage. Brenda had never really liked the Vicarage, and would have preferred a more modern, more convenient home, but she had lived here now for twelve years. Perhaps it was the shock which had made her suddenly once more aware of the decor. She said as much to Grace. Grace agreed with her, but pointed out that she had made it her home and had surely been happy in it.

"Well, yes, that's true," she said. "But we have had our sad times, too."

Grace knew what she meant. Early in their marriage Brenda had miscarried twice. After the second miscarriage, the doctors had told her she could no longer have children. That had been a terrible blow to her and to Graham, who loved children, and would have loved his own. Grace wondered whether it might perhaps prove to be a kind of blessing, since becoming a widow with children might have been even more difficult for Brenda. On reflection she thought this was wrong. Children could never be anything other than a blessing, surely. They were physical evidence of love.

She looked at Brenda, who was staring at a framed wedding photograph on the wall near her. She began to weep, and Grace found herself weeping with her. She was remembering the death of her own husband. She moved over and sat with Brenda, who, at last fell asleep. The only light came from a small lamp in a corner of the room. She left it on and eventually fell asleep herself.

XIV

Peter Hanlon's first major service was the funeral of the man he replaced. The church was packed. Graham Dampier had been well liked. Brenda's sister had come with her three children, who looked bewildered but behaved themselves impeccably.

Brenda herself was composed but pale. Duncan attended the service. He felt it was the least he could do. He sat with Ruth and Grace. He stood with them by the graveside. It was a bright, sunny day, contrasting with the sadness of the ceremony.

Members of the Mothers Union had insisted that they would deal with the catering. The reception was held at the Vicarage. It was as well that the weather was fine, since it would have been impossible for everyone to gather inside. Tables were set up on the lawn, and it began to take on the incongruous appearance of a Church Fete. Since the congregation consisted almost entirely of villagers who knew each other well, conversation was animated and there was even the occasional burst of laughter.

It was, Grace Cole thought, a tribute to the dead man that his funeral proved a distraction from the prevailing mood, which the murders had created. Every day the inhabitants woke with a sense of apprehension. The murderer or murderers had not been caught. They had not even been identified, unless the unpleasant rumours about Duncan were taken in the least seriously. Grace realized such distrust was inspired by fear. When would the police discover the truth? Until that happened, people would continue to conjecture and to blame. So far, all they knew seemed to make little sense. The murders had shaken the very foundations on which the village community was built. She wondered if the damage could ever be made good. Meanwhile, the Vicar's funeral had revived something of the old spirit, even if it was only temporary. Tomorrow, no doubt, all these people in their Sunday best clothes now, would revert to their everyday wear, and also take on the now habitual anxiety. The women were especially uneasy since Peggy

Champion and her son had been attacked in their own home. Now everyone locked their doors at night.

XV

Had the Vicar still been on the Parish Council, Duncan might have known of one more major change. With the introduction of the new Education Act, the County Council was busy building new, so-called, Secondary Modern Schools. The Act was designed to give all children an appropriate secondary education after the age of eleven. The new school in Hazlehurst had now been built and staff recruited. Those children who did not secure a place at the Grammar School by passing the 11+ examination, would now travel by bus from the outlying villages, including Hartsfoot, and attend the new school. This would take effect as from September. Duncan was aware of that much, and hoped that Percy, given the opportunity of joining a new school, might treat it as a more positive adventure. With Duncan's help his work had improved markedly.

What Duncan was not aware of was that Gwen Proctor found the prospect unattractive. She would lose pupils in Percy's age group, leaving her with children between the ages of seven and eleven only. She might have been able to accept that, although it would reduce the number of pupils in the school to a bare minimum, but she was a realist, and it seemed quite likely, from what she had heard from friends and acquaintances in teaching, that the smaller village schools, like the one in Hartsfoot, might well be threatened with closure. She had decided earlier in the year that she would rather jump than be pushed, and she had been applying for other posts. She had been offered and accepted a job as Headteacher of a larger primary school in Hampshire.

She was not unduly dismayed at the thought of leaving Hartsfoot. She had settled in comfortably, and she had generally good relationships with the parents, but her passion was travelling. She spent very little money during term time, spending her energies, instead of her money, on careful and thorough preparation for her work in the school, but the holidays belonged to her. At Christmas she usually went to see her parents or other members of the family, once the traditional Nativity Play was done. If possible, she would set off at Easter in her old Morris 8 on a cheap trip to another part of England. During the summer holidays, provided that the weather was favourable, she would take the ferry from Dover and make her way slowly southwards through France, camping, and spending as little as she could, in order to make her foreign currency allowance stretch. In short, she was conscientious about her job as a teacher, but not wholeheartedly committed to the village itself.

The news of her imminent departure came as a surprise to Duncan halfway through the summer term. Percy's views on the matter were simple: he was glad she was going. Secretly, Percy was also hoping for a new start in a new school. He was beginning to come to terms with some of the work, which hitherto had been so hard for him. He was still not wildly enthusiastic about reading, unless it was reading for a specific purpose. Having found a friend in Duncan, he saw a future for himself as a mechanic, possibly even working for his friend when he was old enough. He knew, because Duncan had told him, that he would need to become good at Maths, and Duncan had explained to him that Maths was not the same as Arithmetic. It was far more interesting than that. Well, he would see, and he had promised Duncan he would try his best.

Duncan, meanwhile, was adding the departure of the schoolteacher to the list of changes that he and Ruth had identified. It had nothing to do with the murders, but then, neither had Graham Dampier's death. The fact was that the entire country seemed to be undergoing a social upheaval. It must surely have something to do with the war. England was still trying to recover from the worst effects. The Armed Forces had equipped many men with skills they would not otherwise have had, but there were fewer men now. So many of them had died. Women, who had taken on the roles normally filled by men, had been displaced again in most cases. Many men, he noted, had opted for a one-year teacher training course, giving them a qualified teacher status, and easing the strain on the new secondary schools.

The newly established National Health Service was a magnificent change for the better. Everyone could quote cases in the past of friends, relatives and acquaintances who had been unable to afford medical attention when it was needed. The old Friendly Societies had been the only way for some people to manage. Now, medical attention was to be free at the point of delivery to everyone. Secondary education was for everyone. West Sussex, unfortunately, had not chosen to build new Technical Schools, but perhaps the so-called Secondary Moderns would provide useful, hands-on training for potential apprentices like Percy. In spite of the continued rationing, there remained hope for the future.

Duncan's own hopes were certainly improving. He had not imagined at any time during the past five years that he would find a woman with whom he could form a close friendship, let alone hope for something closer still. He was determined to tread carefully. Ruth and he got on very well so far. The trial period – three months – would reveal if that compatibility was soundly based. He hoped it was.

XVI

Jack had been shaken by the comments of the Inspector. He might have been charged with handling stolen goods! It was not his fault, he told himself repeatedly, and the fact that he, not original thief, could have accidentally acquired a police record rankled. His mother put his bad mood down to disappointment over the poor experience of a night out. It was not that simple. The following Saturday he announced he was catching the bus into Hazlehurst. Dorothy said she would drive him, but he refused the offer. He didn't mind using the bus, he said, even though it meant a walk into the village. Dorothy shrugged. There were still occasions when she could not understand her son.

Jack had only one thought in mind. He spent the afternoon wandering aimlessly round the small town. He bought a copy of the local paper and spent an hour drinking tea and eating home-made cakes in the tea shop. He was waiting impatiently until six o'clock, when he made his way to the Rising Sun. He was the first customer. The landlord was surprised to see him on his own. He ordered half a pint of bitter and took a seat facing the door. The barman didn't try to make conversation. Jack sipped his drink. He didn't really like it, and would have preferred lemonade, but thought it would look wrong to order a soft drink in a licensed public house.

Other customers arrived in ones and twos. Some of them nodded to Jack by way of greeting. Most ignored him. Two couples came in together and occupied a table near Jack. The women ordered port and lemon. Jack still waited. It was after seven o'clock when Arthur came in. He went straight to the bar, walking with a swagger. When he turned round with a pint of beer in his hand, he looked round the bar to find a seat he fancied.

Jack got up and strode towards him. "I've got a bone to pick with you," he said, word he had been rehearsing.

"Do I know you?"

"You sold me tins of corned beef last week in here."

"Did I? Oh yeah, I remember you now. Can't carry your drink, can you? You looked a bit squiffy."

"Those tins," Jack continued, ignoring him, "were stolen, weren't they?"

Arthur looked at him and his face hardened. "Who says?"

"The police say. They were going to charge me with receiving stolen goods."

"The police? You bloody idiot! You talked to the police?"

"They talked to me. I didn't know the stuff was stolen. I paid you good money."

Arthur laughed, but it was an uncertain laugh. "What the hell did you tell them?"

"The truth. I told them I bought them in this pub from someone called Arthur."

"You bloody fool! You could have put me in it right up to my neck!"

"If I did," said Jack, "it would only be what you deserve."

At this point Arthur swung his arm in anger towards Jack's head. His hand still gripped the handle of the heavy t glass tankard full of beer. If it had collected, it would have created serious damage, even if it did not shatter on impact. As it was, Jack instinctively put out a hand to defend himself. It stopped the blow striking home, but the beer spilt all over him and the floor. He retaliated, throwing a punch which caught Arthur in the chest, causing him to stagger backwards. He roared obscenities, dropped the glass on the floor, where it bounced harmlessly, and launched himself forward to attack Jack in his turn. The two women screamed. The barman and two of the customers stepped forward and pinioned both their arms. Jack and Arthur stared at one another, breathing heavily, angry but restrained. The door opened and a police constable came in, quickly followed by a second. This was their normal, Saturday evening beat. The Rising Sun, they knew, was the most likely source of any trouble, but it didn't normally happen until closing time. They had been lurking around the corner, having a quick cigarette.

"All right! That'll do!" The older of the two policemen spoke. "It's a bit early for this kind of thing, isn't it?" He looked at the two pugilists. "Ah! If it isn't our old friend, Arthur! Arthur White. And here's this here?" He was looking at Jack. "What's your name, son?"

"Jack,"

"Jack what? And where do you come from?"

"Jack Frost. I'm from Hartsfoot."

The policeman looked at his colleague. "There are a couple of decent pubs in Hartsfoot," he said. "Why would anybody want to come to this dump?"

But Jack was not listening. "Did you say Arthur White?" he asked.

"What's it to you?" Arthur was glaring at him.

"Was your father the gamekeeper in Hartsfoot?"

Arthur's eyes narrowed. "Yes," he said. "So what?"

Jack did not reply. He had realized that this was the man he had been wanting to meet, his half-brother. Now he had found him, he was already regretting it.

"Well," said the policeman, "you two had better come with us. Any damage caused?" He was looking at the barman.

"Only beer on the floor. Daresay we can mop that up. He had paid for it."

"Any of you going to tell me what happened?"

But no one wanted to volunteer. By now the immediate anger had cooled. The two policemen led the two pugilists outside. "You can both come down to the station with us," the older man said. "We have to take statements and decide what to do."

"You're not going to charge us?" Jack was beginning to realize the awkwardness of this situation.

"Well, I suppose we could charge you with affray. I doubt if you are both drunk as well as disorderly. When we've got your statements, we'll decide. This way!"

At the police station Jack and Arthur were left for a few moments to sit on a bench facing the Duty Sergeant.

"Is this what you want?" Arthur asked. "You want to get mixed up with the police as well, do you?"

"No. Maybe, if you gave me back my five bob, I'd forget about the whole thing."

"Give you back...? You are even greener than you are cabbage looking."

The policemen took their time. They took a statement from each man, got them to check them through very carefully and sign them. Afterwards they were told in no uncertain terms not to get into any more fights. They were also advised not to frequent the Rising Sun. Then, without more ado, they were allowed to leave.

"Well, thank you for spoiling my night out," Arthur said. "One good thing: you've missed your last bus!"

Indeed, it was nearly 10 o'clock, and the last bus left Hazlehurst at 9:30. Jack was faced with a choice of finding a phone box and asking his mother to come and collect him, or walking. He chose to walk. In any case, he was still trying to accept that this unpleasant spiv-like man and he shared the same genes. At least it was not raining.

He had not reckoned with the possibility of a shower, however. He was still a mile short of Hartsfoot village when it began to rain, and it was a further mile from the Post-Office to the farm. He was drenched when he finally got home. His misery did not end there: his mother, anxious that he had not returned by 10:15, the time it should have taken him to walk from the last bus, was sitting up waiting.

"Jack! Look at the sight of you! Where on earth have you been? Why didn't you phone? Did you miss the bus?"

Jack could not answer this barrage of questions. "I need to dry out," he said and went to the bathroom. There was no hot water: water for the bath had to be heated in a copper, and syphoned into the tub. He towelled himself dry, but Dorothy was waiting when he reappeared, ready with a hot cup of cocoa. This was going to be an uncomfortable night – it was, in fact, after midnight. He was miserable, cold and hungry, and in no mood to talk about his evening. Instead, he ignored the questions, saying he was starving; couldn't everything else wait for the morning. Dorothy produced a cheese sandwich. They both went to bed. Jack slept the dreamless, exhausted sleep of the young; Dorothy lay awake a long time, worrying about this son of hers who kept secrets from her. Was there a girl involved, she wondered. Had he met someone in Hazlehurst, and, if so, why was he so reluctant to admit it? She began imagining scenarios in which Jack was mixed up with a married woman. He was so young, she thought, he could so easily be led astray. At last she, too, drifted off into an uneasy, dream-filled sleep.

Jack had put on working clothes and was heading for the door.

"Where are you going?" Dorothy asked in a tone which brooked no disobedience.

"To work." He turned for a moment, intending to go on.

"Sit down!"

He sat. He looked like a puppy, caught stealing the Sunday lunch.

Dorothy put two cups of tea on the table and sat down to face her son. "You are going to tell me what's going on," she declared. "Who is the girl? There is a girl, isn't there?"

Jack looked at her in genuine astonishment. "Girl?" He said. "What girl? No, there isn't a girl."

Dorothy looked surprised in her turn. She was sure she had worked out the reason for Jack's embarrassment.

"If it wasn't a girl," she said, "what happened?"

Jack looked down at his hands, holding the cup. "I'm sorry, Mum," he said, "I've let you down."

Slowly, stumbling over his words are times, Jack gave an account of the previous afternoon and evening. He had gone into town, he said, with just one thought on his mind, just one intention, and that was to find the man who had tricked him into buying stolen goods and so had got him into trouble with the police. He explained how he had found the man and how, instead of sorting the matter out, he had been involved in an undignified brawl in a public house in Hazlehurst. That itself was enough to make you feel embarrassed and ashamed, but the arrival of the local police and the way in which they had taken him off to the police station was even worse. Dorothy listened, her face stern. She was, she admitted, very upset and disappointed in his behaviour. She was trying to make allowances for the fact that his intentions had been sound enough, but she was finding it difficult.

There was more, said Jack, and, not meeting her eye, he explained that the man with whom he had had a fight, the man called Arthur, had been recognised by the police, and his name was Arthur White.

At the name Dorothy stiffened. "Arthur White, Reubens son?"

"Yes, my brother!"

Then they stared at each other in silence for a few seconds. Dorothy's anger disappeared like a deflated balloon. "I suppose I should have known it might happen," she said. "I should have said something to you before. I just hoped and prayed, probably stupidly, that you would never bump into him. But Hazlehurst is not that far away."

"He's an awful chap!" Jack said. "He may be my brother, but I really hate him!"

"It would have been better if you hadn't met."

"But we have the same father! I could turn out to be like him! They say bad blood runs in the same family, don't they?"

"Oh, Jack! Jack! You will never be like him. You're honest and hard-working. You would never cheat anybody the way he has tricked you. "

"But, if he's my brother, shouldn't I feel better about him?"

Dorothy got up, walked round to her son and kissed him on the top of his head. "You don't have to love someone you don't like," she said. "To all intents and purposes Arthur White is a stranger, just as his father was to you, just as his father really was to me. You are all right as you are, don't doubt yourself. You haven't done anything wrong."

Jack put an arm round her waist then and hugged her. "I hope I'm never anything like him," he said. "If I ever begin to look like that, give me a good kick up the backside."

Dorothy laughed. "I certainly will," she said. "Now, it's Sunday, go and change into some decent clothes. I think we should get away from this place. When you're changing, I'll make some sandwiches and we can go for a picnic."

"A picnic?"

"I never had time to do this when you were a little boy, I always had to get back home when I came to visit you at your auntie's. We'll take a thermos of tea and drive up to the top of Goodwood. It's years and years since I was there. We'll get some lovely clean, Sussex air and, from the very top you can look right down as far as the Isle of Wight. It will do us both good."

XVII

For weeks uncertainty and anxiety hung over Hartsfoot like a cloud. There was still a killer on the loose. Everybody hoped that the Brighton connection meant the murderer had come from that direction. Peggy Champion's experience at the hands of two thugs seemed to confirm that probability. The villagers seized on that as the likely alternative, which was otherwise, God forbid, that the killer was one of their own. Life continued as it had before, but the sense of relief and hope, which had come with the ending of the war, was largely destroyed. No one, not even Martha Brewer, spoke about it, but the lack of apparent progress in the case left the villagers, and especially the women of the village, anxious and apprehensive. Conversations avoided the subject of the murders.

"Mr Frome," said Peggy Champion, stepping into the Forge one afternoon, "I know you've been taking a real interest in Percy's education, so can I ask you something?"

"You can ask, I don't guarantee to know the answer."

"It's this letter," Peggy said, holding out an official looking envelope. "Percy brought it home from school, but I don't really understand it."

Duncan took the envelope from her and opened it. He read the letter carefully. "Percy is not going to like this," he said, "he's going to have to take an exam."

"An exam?"

"Well it's called a test here. You know they've been building a new school in Hazlehurst?"

"Oh, have they?"

"Yes, it's all to do with a new Act of Parliament. All children over the age of eleven will now have to go to a secondary school instead of staying in the same school until the age of fourteen."

"Does that mean that Percy will have to go to the new school?"

"Yes, well, probably."

"I don't understand."

"Sit down. I'll try to explain as much as I know. When they passed this Act of Parliament, all the Local Education Authorities in the country had to make the proper preparations. There weren't enough secondary schools for all children over the age of eleven. It's taken until now for West Sussex to finish building a new school in Hazlehurst. Now all children will have to take a test at the age of eleven to decide if they should go to the new school or, if they're clever enough, to the Grammar School."

"If they are going to the new school, why do they have to take the test?"

"It's just to make sure that the bright children go to the Grammar School."

"So, it won't really matter. Percy will go to the new school, anyway."

Duncan frowned. "You never know," he said. "He really has come on in leaps and bounds this year, you know. It's not just that his readings got better. He wants to be a mechanic, he said, or even an engineer."

"What's the difference?"

Duncan laughed, "I can't begin to explain," he said. "But if Percy really puts his mind to it, this could be quite a chance for him."

Peggy looked thoughtful. "You don't really think he has what it takes, do you?"

"I don't know. I'm not qualified to judge. That's what the test is all about, I suppose."

"Miss Proctor has never thought he was any good at schoolwork, though she did say he had improved this year."

"Well," said Duncan, "Miss Proctor and I do not always agree. She could have been more encouraging. You know she's leaving I suppose?"

"Miss Proctor, leaving? But she's been here for years!"

""It's the new school," Duncan explained. "If the older pupils transferred to the new Secondary Modern or to the Grammar School, the only children left will be those up to the age of eleven. I gather she has found herself another job for next term already."

"Well I never! This village keeps on changing."

That was certainly true, Duncan thought. He had not seriously thought about Percy's chances of getting into the Grammar School. He had no idea what the standards were. Certainly, he had grown to see in Percy signs of intelligent

225

interest, and a surprising willingness to learn. Whether his rapid improvement had come too late was another matter. Time and the test itself would tell.

Peggy left the Forge and walked down the road feeling very uncertain. Duncan's explanation had made her wish that she knew more about all these things herself. Perhaps she could have been more helpful to her son. His father had been no help whatsoever: he had been away at war for several years, and, when he got back, he had shown very little interest in his own son. His bullying ways had left them both in a dark place for much of the time. It was time, maybe, that she, Peggy Champion, took charge of her own life. It might yet be possible for her to provide more support for Percy and, for that matter, for her to start doing things for herself. Maybe she should find out something about evening classes. They might even help her when the little bit of money she had was running out, and she needed to find a job. Not that she would ever be much good at learning.

There were three other children of Jack's age at the school, two girls and another boy. When the test day arrived, several weeks later, a car came to pick up all four children and take them to a school on the outskirts of Hazlehurst. It was a primary school, but much larger than their own. The driver took them to the playground, where a teacher spotted them, and led them into a classroom. There they joined twelve other boys and girls. They were all nervous, quiet, very respectful of the teacher. They sat in separate desks. Each had a pencil and nothing else. The teacher explained what was going to happen.

When he opened the first page of the test, Percy was surprised. It was not like anything he had done before. It was all about words, and it asked him to write sentences with the words in them. There were a number of questions which were really trick questions: afterwards he remembered one of them in which he was given a series of letters and asked what the next letter should be: the letters were, O,T,T,F,F,S,S,E That was easy, and he quickly put down the letter N. Another test, later in the morning, was all about numbers. He found this test not just easy but interesting. He liked numbers now. He found he had really enjoyed it. All the children had a school lunch then, but Percy was surprised to find that most of them had not enjoyed the tests at all. His three friends from Hartsfoot were quite gloomy in the car going home, but Percy was bursting with excitement, and dashed straight into the Forge to tell Mr Froom all about it. He stopped when he realized that Miss Cole was in there with Mr Frome. They were both drinking tea.

"Hello, Percy," said Mr Frome. "How did you get on?"

Percy looked from one to the other, a little uncertain.

"Your test, I mean."

"Mr Frome has been telling me all about it," said Miss Cole. "Was it awful?"

"No," Percy said. "It was jolly good fun."

"Fun? Gosh! I hated doing tests myself," said Miss Cole.

"That's what the girls said in the car," said Percy, "but I enjoyed it. I didn't know what to expect. It wasn't like ordinary school stuff."

"Good for you."

Miss Cole poured out a mug of tea and handed it to him. He was a bit surprised but sat down and told them all about it. The two adults listened, showed interest, asked questions, he quite liked Miss Cole, he decided, even if she did have her eye on Mr Frome.

PART FOUR

Brave New World

I

Whatever his shortcomings, and they were many, The Bear was extremely thorough. He and his team would follow up the faintest of clues, even if it seemed to be leading nowhere. Perhaps one of the advantages of lacking imagination was that The Bear was able to concentrate on detail. He just liked to be busy. It did not matter to him what the outcome of any line of enquiry was. It was rewarding on those rare occasions when the outcome was positive; for the rest of the time he was content simply to explore. When he had spotted the tins of corned beef in Dorothy Frost's kitchen, he had only expected to identify the supply chain which Joe White was linked with. He did not like black marketeers. They provided goods which were in short supply, and did so illegally, charging high prices as they navigated their cunning ways around the law. He took a similarly poor view of those members of the public who bought black market goods. They were, in his view, conniving with criminals. In the case of Dorothy Frost, she was only partly involved: it was her stupid, young son who had bought the goods. Of far more interest to The Bear was how Joe White had obtained the stuff in the first instance.

He looked at the tins. There was nothing very remarkable about them, but there was a code, a serial number, stamped on the bottom of the tin. He assumed this was a batch number and, if it proved possible to contact the factory that produced it or, failing that, the agent who had imported it, he might be able to trace it. It was a typically boring task for someone. It was also the kind of task which his team was used to. It took several weeks.

There seemed to be a great deal about this case which involved foodstuffs. The involvement of the gamekeeper in providing illicit venison, which had been sold in Brighton, led to the Brighton CID, as did the contents of the box which Peggy Champion had handed in. The scribbled drawings and notes at the bottom of that box provided extremely useful evidence of this gang's activities. They were clearly a versatile bunch: they had carried out many burglaries over a wide area in the past two years. They had also, through Joe Champion's contact, managed to poison a lot of people with meat, which had been prepared by an unlicensed butcher, that is, by Reuben White. The Bear, who was kept in close touch by the Brighton CID, was not himself involved in investigating the gang. He had to bear in mind that the murders in The Chase were his primary concern, but it was very possible that a member or members of the gang were responsible for the deaths. He had no evidence one way or another on that score.

He was a patient man. He had been given limits within which he could work. The destruction of the bunker, together with the compulsion to keep it secret, had cut off a very wide area of possible investigation. He was left with the people of the village. In spite of the antagonism towards the victims, none of these people seemed to have a motive to kill both Reuben White and Joe Champion. Both had been killed, using the same weapon. It was still a mystery why Joe Champion had also been shot with the pistol. Ballistics had confirmed that the pistol they had retrieved from the bunker had fired the shot which killed Joe Champion. Why had someone shot him twice? Or – and this was a distinct possibility – were there two people involved? The killing had all the hallmarks of an execution, suggesting the gang might be responsible.

There were several food-processing plants which produced corned beef. Much was imported from Argentina, but three factories in England also produced the stuff. It was under strict control , not only for hygiene reasons, but because meat was rationed. All three factories were very reluctant to give any information. It was only when the words 'murder enquiry' were employed that there was co-operation. The third contact confirmed that the code on the bottom of the tins was theirs. The letters and numbers referred to the date and time the tins had been filled, and the last three characters were the order number.

"Good!" said the sergeant who was on the telephone. "Can you please now check the order in question and tell me where it was sent?"

The woman on the other end of the line asked him to wait while she checked the files. It took several minutes.

"I'm sorry," she said at last, "I can't tell you."

"Can't tell me? Why? Lost the records?"

"No. We've got the records, We are not allowed to tell you/"

"Not allowed? But I've already explained, this is part of a murder investigation. Who says you can't tell us?"

"I can't say."

"That's ridiculous. Can I speak to your manager?"

"He'll tell you the same. I can only tell you it was a Government Ministry."

"Was it, indeed? Which Ministry?"

But he got no more. He reported to The Bear.

"Are you thinking what I'm thinking, boss?"

"MI5!" The enquiry was haunted by security issues. The two men sat in the Inspector's office in silence for a while, until the Sergeant, said, "You don't think this corned beef has anything to do with the bunker, do you?"

"Do you remember the stock of food and water in the bunker?"

"Yes, and there were tins of bully beef, I remember."

The Bear nodded.

"No way we can find out now" the Sergeant said resignedly. "Absolutely everyone seems sworn to secrecy."

"We'll just have to tackle it from the other end," said The Beer. "Ger Arthur White back."

"He hasn't been very helpful so far."

"Perhaps we can put the fear of God into him."

The Sergeant was puzzled. He frowned to show he didn't understand.

"We don't know where he got this stuff from, but we can bluff him, tell him it was part of a special consignment for the Secret Service. He won't know any better, but we can talk about breaches of security and heavy penalties."

It all sounded too fanciful for the Sergeant, but he knew better than to put more obstacles in the way. Bluffing was what the Inspector did. Arthur White would be brought in.

II

When Mervyn Hardcastle chaired the next meeting of the Parish Council, it was obvious that he was not his normal self. The usual, jovial man had turned into a serious, unsmiling one. He lost his way in the agenda. He had already forgotten the names of the two newcomers, and had to apologise to them, when he welcomed them. Mrs Crabtree, the Secretary, threw sharp, enquiring glances in his direction as the meeting proceeded. When, uncharacteristically, he lost his place in the agenda, she asked him outright, "Is anything the matter, Mr Hardcastle?"

"I'm so sorry," he said. "You, of course, know of my involvement with the Estate. I had to declare it as a possible conflict-of-interest might occur, when I first joined the Parish Council. I suppose you have all heard about the scandal involving our Estate Manager."

There were nods around the table. "Something about theft , wasn't it?" Matthew Stevens said.

"Yes. He is under investigation by the police. Since I am a Board member, and I live close to our office in Hazelhurst, it has fallen to me to deal with the day-to-day business of the Estate myself. I do apologise, but I'm finding it difficult to concentrate on this evening's matters. I'm having to do all the accounts for the Estate myself at the moment."

"That must mean a considerable amount of work," Mrs Crabtree observed. "I imagine you are looking to recruit a new Estate Manager."

"Yes, but these things take time."

"Have you anyone who does the bookkeeping for you?"

"At the moment, no. That is part of the question."

"Have you thought of speaking to Mrs Dampier?"

"Brenda Dampier? Why should I speak to Brenda?"

"Maybe you don't know," Mrs Crabtree explained, "but Brenda is an experienced bookkeeper. Before she married Graham, she was the Diocesan Secretary. She worked for the Diocese for several years."

Mervyn Hardcastle was interested, as, indeed were the other members of the Parish Council, listening to this dialogue.

"Thank you for the suggestion, Mrs Crabtree," Mervyn said. "I shall have a word with her." And he returned to the agenda with renewed vigour.

He wasted no time; the very next morning he visited the Vicarage, where he found Brenda in the office, helping the new curate sort some of the documents in the desk. When he said he would like to speak to her privately, she led him to the kitchen and made drinks. They sat at the small table. Brenda was composed, but still showed signs of strain. Mervyn realized she must feel very uncertain about the future as well as grieving for her husband.

"I believe," he said, "that you used to work for the Bishop as an accountant."

"I was more a bookkeeper than an accountant," Brenda said. "I was actually Secretary. I admit I enjoyed it. I've been thinking I might even find similar work in the future. I shall have to move out of here sometime; the Vicarage belongs to the Church, and the next Vicar may well have a family to house."

" Well, then, let me explain. I'm sure you will know about the unfortunate affair of the Estate Manager. I have had to dismiss him, of course. For the moment I am doing my best to cope with the administration of the Estate, but I need to appoint a new Manager. It is largely an administrative job, but it obviously needs someone who can keep track of our accounts. Do you think it could be something you could deal with??"

"It sounds like a very important job."

"I suppose it is quite important. The question is, could you manage it and, if so, would you want to do it?"

"I'm always open to a challenge," said Brenda, "but I would need to know a lot more."

"That's very good. Perhaps, if I sent a car for you, you might spend the day in the Office with me. It will take at least a day to explain things, and we may have to start a whole new system to replace the one used by Scrivener. This is quite urgent, so, if you could see your way clear to meeting me in, say, three or four days' time, give me a ring."

Brenda looked thoughtful, it sounded like a very big challenge, but it would provide her with an income. She was going to need an income, as well as having to find a new home.

"I forgot to say," Mervyn added, "the Estate Office is part of the Manager's accommodation. You would have the use of the house as a personal home. It's rather more modern than this Vicarage, but it is quite tastefully decorated." He smiled a little, bitter smile. " I suspect that Scrivener made sure the Estate paid for a high standard of decoration."

Brenda thought seriously about the offer, when she had seen him out. If the task of managing the Estate was within her capabilities, it could mean a new start for her, returning to the kind of work she had enjoyed at the Diocesan Office. She was reasonably confident that her skills would be adequate. Provided the general administration was something she could cope with, this would provide her with accommodation as well as an income.

Her sister, being tactful, did not comment on Brenda's sudden change of mood, but was surprised that she seemed more positive about the future, rather than miserably nostalgic.

III

Peter Hanlon, the new Curate, was a young man. He was polite and respectful towards Brenda, recognising her pain in bereavement. He had been injured during the war, and had been invalided out of the Army. He had immediately begun his training for the church. He had plenty of ideas, some of which sounded almost bizarre to Brenda. One of his enthusiasms was music – not the traditional, Victorian hymn tunes – nor, for that matter, other traditional church music. He played the piano-accordion and was keen on country dancing.

One of his first ventures was to advertise a new Youth Club. It was to meet in the church on Wednesday evenings. He wrote out several copies of his notice on cards, and these he posted on the Parish noticeboard and other places in the village, including the pub, the public phone box, and, ignoring Martha's frowns of disapproval, in the window of the Post-Office. Three teenage boys and four girls turned up to the first session. They presented Peter with ideas of their own, including table-tennis, but they joined in square dances and the Club rapidly grew.

Older members of the congregation disapproved. They were not in favour of the playing of anything other than 'sacred music', and found dancing close to profane. As the weeks went by, however, and the Club grew, they acknowledged that the young Curate was at least bringing young people into the church. They were surprisingly polite to the older members, and they seemed to be aware of problems in the wider world. They were interested in collecting money for charities and for such things as helping the thousands of Displaced Children, most of whom were war orphans. They even seemed ready to build bridges with former enemies, including the Germans.

Brenda kept house for the Curate, but she soon accepted Mervyn's offer to work as his Estate Manager on a three-months' trial. Being thus involved in activities, which were as enjoyable as they were demanding, helped her deal with her grief. As the three months passed, it was clear she was more than capable of handling the work. Her experience as a Vicar's wife was a definite asset when she had to deal with Estate tenants, some of them tenant farmers. She soon began to feel a confidence and a sense of purpose that were quite new.

A replacement Vicar was appointed. Brenda was, all at once, overwhelmed by the work involved in moving house. Combined with the demands of the new job, it would have been even more burdensome, had not Grace Cole volunteered to help. Together they sorted and packed or disposed of the many belongings that had been accumulated over the years. Ruth, too, helped from time to time. The young Curate was willing enough to lend his muscles to move large boxes and even pieces of furniture.

Secretly, Grace arranged a surprise farewell party in the Village Hall. She spread the news through the WI, but other women wanted to join in. Some men also turned up on the day. Brenda, taken unawares, spent most of the afternoon in tears, although, as many reminded her, she was only moving three miles away. She had not realized for one moment she was so loved by the people of the village.

For those villagers that she was leaving, there was the prospect of a new Vicar. Gwen Proctor had already moved on to Hampshire at Easter. The village had changed. But, the unease, and underlying fear remain all the time that there was a murderer on the loose.

IV

"You? Suspect?" Ruth stood up on the other side of the bonnet. She had a grease mark on one cheek, her hair was wispy and untidy. The boiler suit she wore was too large for her, and she had rolled up the sleeves. Duncan found her attractive all the same.

"Well, it's true," he said. "You might not have noticed, but he didn't contradict that chap when he all but name me as the murderer."

"But he was drunk, was taken?"

"I don't think he was drunk, but he had been drinking. The trouble is, other people listen to him."

"You don't think they believed him?"

"Oh, they didn't really need to believe him. The suspicion is bad enough. I'm an outsider in this village. It's hard enough just to get accepted. I've never really thanked you for what you said in my defence."

"It wasn't entirely in your defence," she said. "I just don't like so many prejudiced ideas being flung about. I don't like the way this village is ready to accuse innocent people."

"They are worried," Duncan said. "Two murders, and no arrests. Of course, they're worried."

"Isn't time for a fag?" Ruth said. "I'm dying for one."

Duncan agreed and they adjourned to the workshop to make a cup of tea. Duncan was not only conscious of the growing attraction he felt for Ruth, but also of the fact that her three-month trial period was coming to an end. He looked at her and realized he would miss her if she were to leave.

"You realize," Ruth said, "that the three months are nearly up?"

"Yes. I'm waiting to find out what you've decided."

"Well, we seem to get along together. I certainly am enjoying learning from you. You're a good teacher."

"That's very flattering," he said. "Does that mean?" He left the question unfinished.

"There is certainly plenty going on in the village at the moment," Ruth said. "I still miss some of the things I enjoyed in Luton. It would be nice to get dressed up from time to time and go out somewhere for the evening. I still find it quiet here."

"So, you will be moving on?"

"I didn't say that." Ruth drew on her cigarette and blow out a large cloud of smoke. She was frowning in concentration. "I really would like to stay, I think. I'm not sure that I want to be living in such a quiet place with no distractions. It's like being old before my time."

"Well," Duncan said, "what about a compromise?"

"Compromise? How can there be a compromise? The job is here, not in town."

"But it's not the job that's the problem, is it? It's the leisure time, the chance to get out and enjoy things."

"Yes, I suppose that's it. There's not a lot to do in Hartsfoot in the evenings."

"Well, here's the compromise. There is nothing at all to prevent you from visiting friends, even friends in Luton, except getting there. What if I paid you a bonus to enable you to, say, spend a long weekend with your friends every month? And, if you are happy to accept something less, how would you feel about my taking you out to the occasional dance in, say, Woodbury?"

"You'd do that?"

"Yes, I would. I haven't said this properly, but I have grown more than fond of you over the past few weeks. I know

242

you may consider me to be second-hand goods, so to speak, having been married before...."

"Second-hand goods! What an extraordinary thing to say! I had never thought of you in that way! I like your, I've never disguised the fact."

"You may change your mind. I'm not sure 'like' is the word that describes how I feel. It's a bit stronger than that. In fact, I am feeling confused. I think I'm beginning to fall for you."

Ruth looked at him, studying his face before she replied.

"I'm glad we're being honest with one another," she said. "I think we both realize there is a mutual attraction here. I'll stay, but I'm not sure about this bonus idea. If I want to go away for a weekend to see my friends, I don't see why you should have to pay for it."

"It would be worth it, just to have you stay."

"I'll stay anyway," she said. "But as for the, the other thing, let's take it slowly. We began as friends, and I don't want to lose that."

"That's good enough for me," said Duncan. He stood up to collect the empty mugs, and was surprised when Ruth also stood, and, slipping an arm around his neck, pulled his head down and kissed him warmly. This time, for the first time, it was a long, lingering, lovers' kiss. They held each other close for a few moments, then returned to their work. Except for a few essential instructions and requests to pass spanners or other tools, they did not speak for the next half hour, although, from time to time, they exchanged glances and smiles.

V

"I want to know," said The Bear, "where you got these tins of corned beef?"

"Are you joking?" Arthur White had no intention of answering the question.

"I am deadly serious. I don't think you realize, but there are marks on the tins." He turned one of the tins over and pointed to the code stamped into the metal. "These few letters are there for a purpose. They tell us who supplied these tins in the first instance."

Arthur looked disconcerted. "I don't know where they came from," he said, "I just bought them from a chap who said they were Army surplus supplies."

"Pull the other one," said The Bear. "It's got bells on. I'll bet you can't give me the name of this mythical man."

"Well I wouldn't want to drop him in it, would I?"

"You sound like a journalist who wants to protect his sources. That won't wash, young man. Now, where did you get these tins?"

"I told you, I bought them. They were cheap."

"That is a pack of lies. You didn't buy them at all, did you?"

"I did."

"Right," said The Bear, sitting back in his seat, steepling his hands in front of him, tapping the fingers together. "I'll level with you. This foodstuff came from a very special place, so special, that anyone who had unauthorised access to it would be likely to be charged with espionage."

Arthur White sat upright at this point, startled by the information. "What're you talking about?"

"I told you, these tins can only have been acquired by someone breaking into a secure place, a secret place protected by the Official Secrets Act. Anyone who had anything to do with it may be charged with stealing official secrets. That's the same as spying, and that's the same as treason. You are, I suppose, aware of the penalty for treason?"

Arthur White looked totally bemused. He did not at first reply. The Bear waited.

Uncertainly, Arthur said, "You're bluffing."

The Bear heard the uncertainty in his voice. He closed in on his prey. "I told you," he said, "these few letters and numbers, printed on the bottom of these tins, are very significant. We have spent a long time tracing them. I'm giving you some idea of what we have discovered. If you want to save your skin, I suggest you take the opportunity to tell me now where you got them from. And don't give me any of that bullshit about buying them from a friend or something. And I am, I repeat, deadly serious about the possible penalties of trying to hide the truth."

Arthur licked his lips. He was beginning to sweat. The Bear waited again.

"I got them from my dad," Arthur said at last.

"From your dad?" The Bear did not look convinced.

"Yes. I don't know where he got them from."

"You are trying to tell me that your father, who, of course, can no longer contradict you, kindly gave or sold you this food?"

"Yes."

"This is the father who, you told me, treated you badly as a child, the man you did not want to live with, so much so that you preferred to pay for lodgings, when you could have had a free bed in his cottage? The man with whom you were on such bad terms that you broke into his cottage to steal money from him. Yet, you are trying to tell me that he gave you this stuff? Are you saying that he sold it to you so cheaply that you can make a profit at two and six?"

"All right," Arthur admitted, "so, I stole them from him."

"That's closer to the truth, but it's not the whole truth, is it?"

"What do you mean by that?"

"Exactly where did your father keep this stuff, which you say you stole? I am absolutely certain that it was not in his cottage."

"Where else would it be?"

"That is the point. You tell me the truth, or the matter will be taken out of my hands. I can't tell you what the outcome of that would be, but I've given you some idea. If I were you, I would take this opportunity to tell the truth. It might go in your favour."

Arthur White was shaken. He did not want to reveal the entire truth of the matter. He sensed that The Bear was steering him into a trap, but he could not see any way to avoid it. The Bear continued to stare at him accusingly. He was closing in for the kill.

"All right," Arthur admitted at last, "if you must know, my dad had a sort of hideout in The Chase. It was like an underground room, a dug-out. I don't know what it was for."

"How did you find out about it?"

" I told you. I'm good at keeping out of sight in the woods. I learned all about that as a kid. I got curious when I came back from the war, wondering what my dad was up to in The Chase, why he was so keen to frighten everybody, so they never went near it. It was easy enough for me to look around without being seen. I only went two or three times, but I saw him kill a deer, skin it and take the carcass back to the cottage. Another time I saw him do something weird; he went to place near the big clearing, and he bent over and opened a kind of trapdoor. Then he went down inside. I went back to the same place once and I found this trapdoor. It was made of iron, very heavy. I had to have a look, didn't I? I didn't stay very long because I was scared he would come back while I was down there, but I didn't think he would notice if I pinched a couple of tins of corned beef. That's where I got them."

The Bear was enjoying himself. It was as though he was engaging in the endgame of a game of chess. He broke off the interview so that Arthur White could make a formal statement in which he had admitted that he knew of the bunker and had entered it. Now he was trapped. One, or possibly two more moves would end in checkmate. To Arthur's consternation he was not allowed to leave after signing his statement. Instead he was taken to a police cell where, he was told, he would remain while they "carried out further investigations".

The following morning, he was led from the cell back to the interview room.

"You have admitted entering the underground bunker," The Bear began.

Arthur White was looking decidedly more nervous this time. He said nothing, but his bravado had gone, and he looked vulnerable. The Bear moved in for the kill.

"I believe you removed more than just a few tins of corned beef."

Arthur looked very wary. "No," he said, "there wasn't much else there worth pinching and, in any case, I was in too much of a hurry. I was scared dad might come back and find me there."

The Bear turned to a small table and removed a box file. He placed it in front of him and opened it. "Do you recognise this?" he asked, and he took from the file the pistol with its silencer, placing it on the table immediately in front of Arthur. Arthur's reaction was instantaneous. His whole body stiffened, and his head snapped back as though he had been given a sudden, electric shock.

"What is it?" He asked.

"You know perfectly well what it is. It's the pistol which you used to shoot Joe Champion. We retrieved the bullet from Joe Champion's body. No one else had access to that bunker. You are the only person who could possibly have taken this weapon, used it, wiped it clean of your fingerprints, and dropped it back inside the bunker, where we found it."

Arthur knew the game was up. It took very little further persuasion for him to describe exactly what had happened on that fatal evening.

"It was self-defence," he said.

"Self-defence? How do you make that out?"

"I was in the – what did you call it? – bunker?" The Bear nodded. "I didn't even know that dad was going to be in The Chase. He must have come in after I got there. I wanted to know what was down there, you see. I suppose you've worked out that I must've gone back later to pinch the tins of meat?"

The Bear nodded. "Yes. But you didn't know was that I had been down there. I saw the supplies on the shelf. It was a bit later, when people came to empty the place, that I realized some of the tinned meat was missing. One of the things that policemen are trained to do is to be observant."

"Well," Arthur continued, "I didn't have much time on that night to look around. I just got to the bottom when I heard voices. One of them was dad, the other I didn't know, but it

249

turned out to be Joe Champion. They were arguing loudly. I didn't know what it was about, but I wanted to get out of there quickly. I'd picked up this gun because it looks so weird with this attachment on the barrel."

"It's a silencer," The Bear explained.

"Oh, that's what it is! I wondered why it made a funny coughing noise, not a loud bang. Anyway, I still had it in my hand when I climbed out of the dugout. It was only a few steps away from the clearing. But I expect you remember that. I had just got out when I heard a shot. I ran a few steps as far as the clearing. Joe Champion had just shot my father. He still had the shot gun in his hand. He heard me coming and he turned towards me. I didn't really think about it, I was too scared. I just pointed the gun at him and pulled the trigger. It made this sort of coughing noise and he fell backwards. He would have shot me if I hadn't shot first."

"So, how come that both barrels of his gun had been fired? Why was he shot with a shot gun?"

"I realized I must've killed him. I swear to God it was because I thought he was going to shoot me, but, once I'd done it, I realized I could be charged with murder. I don't want to hang! I thought the best thing to do was to make out that they had killed each other, so I picked up his shot gun and shot him again. I just thought…"

The Bear nodded. "You did your best to mislead the police," he said. "You wiped the fingerprints off the shot gun. That made it instantly obvious that Joe Champion was not the last person to fire it. Not very clever, was it?"

"No. I thought, if I didn't wipe fingerprints off, it would look even worse for me."

"Well, it doesn't look all that good for you now, does it? We spent weeks getting to this point. You must have known we'd found the pistol, because you went back, didn't you?"

"I went back to get it later, after you had done your investigating in The Chase. I didn't know you'd found the dugout place, and I thought it might be best to take that gun anyway. But it wasn't there. Everything else looked the same. I grabbed a couple of tins of bully beef and scarpered. I never went back again."

"That bunker really was top secret," the Bear said. "I don't know what charges you are going to face over that. I am now going to charge you with murder." Before Arthur could reply, he cautioned him.

A short while later, as he was about to make a full report to the Superintendent, he wondered whether Arthur White would escape the death penalty, in view of his claim that he had shot Joe Champion in self defence. A good lawyer might pull it off, and the charge could be reduced to manslaughter, but the stupidity of Arthur's actions, following the shooting, the way in which he had misled the police, denied any kind of responsibility, wasted police time – he might avoid the hangman's noose, but he would surely spend a very long time in jail.

VI

Grace Cole had continued to keep an eye on Peggy. Now that the Brighton gang had been discovered and the members charged with various crimes, including GBH on the part of the two thugs who had attacked her and her son, Peggy felt less vulnerable. Grace felt some degree of responsibility for her, especially now that Brenda Dampier had taken on a new role in Hazelhurst. Grace broached a delicate subject.

"I hope you don't mind my asking," she said, "but are you going to be all right for money?"

"It will be a bit of a struggle," Peggy admitted, "but I have the money that your Mr Frome gave me for the car. That will last a while. I was thinking of getting myself a job, but I don't have any qualifications. Maybe I should look for a course, evening classes or something. I should try to keep up with Percy." She said it with a smile, but Grace saw she was serious.

"That sounds like a good idea," she said, "but he's not *my* Mr Frome, not yet, at least.."

Peggy gave her a quizzical look. "Not yet?"

"I think romance is in the air for the two of them."

The two women smiled like indulgent parents.

"Won't the Army provide you with a pension?" Grace returned to the subject.

"That's what Mr Frome said, but I told him I hadn't a clue how to find out. He said I should find Joe's old pay book and he would help me. So, I searched everywhere I could think, and I found it. It was no use."

""Why not?"

"I didn't know, but I soon found out why Joe had been demobbed so early. It said he had been 'dishonourably discharged'. He must have been up to no good even while he was in the Army. They got rid of him as soon as the war was over."

Grace took in the information without replying for a few minutes, then, "He really was a useless husband," she said.

Peggy nodded dumbly. They sipped their tea and contemplated the frailties of men.

They were interrupted by someone knocking on the front door. Peggy went to open it. The Inspector stood on the doorstep. He raised his hat. "May I come in?"

Reluctantly, Peggy stood aside and led the way to the sitting room. The Bear said good morning to Grace. The two women looked at him with little sign of welcome.

"What I have to tell you is personal," said The Bear. "Can we speak privately?"

"Mrs Cole is a very good friend," said Peggy. "You can tell me whatever it is with her present. Don't tell me there's more bad news."

"No, just the opposite," The Bear said, sitting down, uninvited. "I have not one but two pieces of good news for you. The first is that we now know who killed your husband, and he has been charged with his murder."

"Who?"

"It was Arthur White."

"Arthur White?" Both women were astonished.

"But it was Arthur's father who was killed!" Grace was bewildered.

The Bear explained the sequence of events. Both Grace and Peggy were shocked.

"That's terrible," Grace said. "Are you saying that Arthur White witnessed the murder of his own father, and then murdered Joe?"

"Exactly, just that.!

They were having trouble taking this in...

"I said I had two pieces of news," The Bear continued. He paused.

"I'm not sure I want to hear any more." Peggy was looking dazed.

"I think you will want to hear this. You remember that we were tracing where the contents of that box you discovered came from?"

"All that money! And those lovely jewels! I hope they've gone back to their rightful owners."

"Yes, we managed to trace almost all of them. Those scribbled notes you may remember helped identify the places that had been burgled."

"I'm glad," Peggy said.

"The really good news," The Bear said, clearly enjoying the moment, "is that many of the larger items of jewellery were insured, and the insurance company had offered a reward for their recovery. I'm pretty sure you will get a substantial sum."

"But that can't be right!" Peggy protested. She could not believe this good fortune. "It was my husband who helped steal them."

"But it was you who handed them in, and you helped us track down all the other thieves. No one thinks you are in any way to blame for your husband's crimes"

When he left, the two women sat and talked. The "substantial sum" had not been quantified, but the Inspector thought it was probably at least £1,000. It might well ease Peggy's situation, especially now her son, unexpectedly, appeared likely to be going to the grammar school in Hazelhurst. That would involve expense. Fortunately, Percy was at school that morning. It was his last year in the village school. The new, male teacher was much more to his liking than Miss Proctor ever was.

VII

The village, Martha Brewer thought, as she served yet another stranger, wasn't the same anymore. A lot of it, she concluded, was down to Duncan Frome and his ambitious plans. The new building next door dominated the main street. There were now three petrol pumps where once there had been just one. They had even erected some huge canopy thing which was lit up at night. The new building was all plate glass windows, out of keeping with the rest of the village. There was noise from the workshop, less than she had expected, and a lot of it came from the motorcyclists. They came because Duncan Frome seemed to be good at mending bikes. Funny to think he had started out by doing up old bikes. Even the first lot of motorbikes had been second-hand, not like now. She still didn't like the noise they made. And with the new pumps, the garage was busy selling petrol. Jenny had a very full-time job. As well as all that, they seemed to be very busy dealing with repairs and with maintaining vans that belonged to the Estate, and vehicles from the local farmers. Duncan Frome had been obliged to take on another, full-time mechanic as well as Ruth Cole. Ruth Cole! Martha could not honestly approve of a woman working in that kind of occupation, up to her elbows in oil and grease; what was she thinking of?

There was, she admitted grudgingly, a knock-on benefit to be had from Duncan Frome's business success: her little Post Office was much busier than before. There was, or seemed to be, a constant stream of customers these days. The stock was turning over very fast and she was rushed off her feet much of the time. Indeed, she was beginning to wonder whether she should take on an assistant. There was so little space behind the counter, that would be very difficult. Maybe things had been better when they were quieter.

There had been a great deal of notoriety for the village when the murders had occurred, and even more when Arthur White had been charged with murder. Imagine that! The trial, which was planned to take place next month, would be splashed in all the papers, including the national press. At least the villagers could now sleep easy in their beds, but nowadays everyone made sure their doors were locked.

It would be very strange in two years' time when the school closed for good. It was already different, because the older children now caught the bus every morning into Hazelhurst. And young Percy Champion looked quite smart in his new cap and blazer. Who would have thought it? Percy, the son of a criminal, a criminal who had been shot dead, murdered in The Chase.

And the dear old Vicar also dead and buried, Brenda, his wife, back at work and living in Hazelhurst! The new Vicar was a bachelor, sharing the Vicarage with that young Curate fellow, the one who played cheap, modern music in the church!

There weren't many of the old inhabitants whose lives had not been changed. Martha tried to do a mental rollcall. There was a little lull: there hadn't been a single customer for the past twenty-five minutes. Grace Cole, now, she was one of the old ones. She hadn't changed much, though it was Grace who had taken Duncan Frome in as a lodger. Martha wasn't sure that was a good idea, and it was especially thought-provoking now that Ruth was living under the same roof. Not only did she work with Duncan Frome, from the way they behaved, there was obviously something going on between them. Plenty of room for suspicion there! Her sister, Emily, had produced a baby boy last month and Grace never stopped bragging about it.

No, things were not the same. Was this what we had fought the war for? When would rationing ever end? She was heartily sick of having to cut out those silly little coupons.

The Post Office door opened, and Mr Hardcastle came in. Martha smiled at him. Mr Hardcastle was a real gentleman. He had done a lot for the village. The village cricket club now met in his little field. He bought a dozen first-class stamps.

"Tell me Miss Brewer," he said, "what is your opinion about having street- lights in the village?"

"That would be a good idea," she said, "as long as they didn't shine in people's windows at night, like that monstrosity next door."

""Most people seem to agree with you. Perhaps the Parish Council can get something done soon."

Yes, she thought, as he raised his hat and said good day, some changes might be for the better.

THE END